Who is a friend indeed?

*

HARVEY LIVINGSTON: Harvey always expected other people to provide "reasonable explanations." Now he thought Karen should explain just why her husband had vanished with a fortune.

*

LYDIA VANDERGREIT: With her molasses-like Southern cloying Lydia could be obnoxious in the best of times. Now that she was trying to keep Karen's spirits up it was altogether unbearable.

*

IAN FELTHAM: Because the missing secretary was his fiancée, he came to Karen as a partner in distress. But he was soon accusing Karen's missing husband of murder.

*

JILL DERWENT: Karen's cousin was in town for a matinée. Just when Karen needed her most, Jill fell in love with the murdered woman's fiancé.

*

SIMONE CONWAY: "You are not understanding me," the Chief Accountant and wife of the company's best salesman kept saying to Karen. And the more Karen watched Simone in action, the more she agreed.

★   ★   ★

"BOOKS OF MARVELLOUS VERSATILITY AND FRESHNESS...[WITH] FLASHES OF DELICIOUS HUMOR....MARIAN BABSON'S CRIME NOVELS HAVE GONE FROM STRENGTH TO STRENGTH."
—*Twentieth Century Crime and Mystery Writers*

"A WRITER WHO NEVER DISAPPOINTS."
—*Rave Reviews*

MARIAN BABSON

THERE MUST BE SOME MISTAKE

WARNER BOOKS

A Time Warner Company

WARNER BOOKS EDITION

Cover illustration by Phil Singer
Cover design by Jackie Merri Meyer

This Warner Books Edition is published by arrangement with St. Martin's Press, 175 Fifth Avenue, New York, N.Y. 10010.

Warner Books, Inc.
1271 Avenue of the Americas
New York, NY 10020

 A Time Warner Company

Printed in the United States of America

First Warner Books Printing: July, 1993

10 9 8 7 6 5 4 3 2 1

CHAPTER 1

EVERYONE was so very kind. Perhaps that was the hardest thing to bear.

"Of course, *we* don't believe it for one little minute." Lydia had been the first to telephone.

"*We* simply can't take it in," Lydia drawled, her "*we*" not only royal, but universal, encompassing not just herself and her husband, the Chairman of the Board, but the entire multinational company he represented and all its offshoots. One of which was now Harding Handicrafts, which had been taken over two years ago, and which had spent most of the ensuing time in a desperate struggle to attempt to retain its own identity instead of allowing the company to wrestle it into an appropriate corporate slot.

"*We* know that it simply can't be true," Lydia went on, her voice growing more Southern Belle-ish and Dixieland by the syllable, until one began to feel that one was slipping, sliding, drowning in a soft morass of thick cloying molasses. "There has just been some awful, terrible mistake."

1

"Yes," Karen agreed faintly.

"That's right, honey," Lydia applauded. "You just keep your spirits up. Why, I'll bet you, just any time now, John will show up at the door—and he'll have an explanation for *everything*. And then won't we all feel silly billies for doubting him for one little minute!"

"Yes," Karen said again. Until now, she had not believed that it might be true. Lydia's insistent understanding bludgeoned at the weak defences she had not realized she had erected, and she sensed them crumbling.

"Listen, honey—" Lydia's ear had evidently caught the first faint cracking of the wall. "Is there anything I can do? Any little old thing at all—?"

"No!" Karen caught at her slipping control. "No, thank you. It's quite all right—*I'm* quite all right."

"Honey, don't be so *English*. This is *me*—Lydia. I'm your friend, remember?"

"I remember," Karen said. Instant friendship—that was what Lydia and Vernon Vandergreit specialized in. She and John had often laughed at it, betting between themselves on the instant forgetfulness that would ensue when one of Lydia and Vernon's "friends" turned in his resignation and departed to work for another firm.

"Honey," Lydia probed, "are you alone there? I mean, is anyone with you right now? I can come over right away. You shouldn't have to see this through alone. I can be there in ten minutes—"

"No!" Karen said. "That is, it's frightfully kind of you, Lydia. But, actually, I was planning to meet my Cousin Jill in town for a matinee, and I—I see no reason to change my plans. As you've said, this is all some kind of misunderstanding—"

"Well, I think it's just wonderful of you to take it like this, honey." Lydia seemed not to notice that she was reversing herself. "Carrying on, regardless. That's that old British spirit that we all know and love—"

"I really must go now, Lydia." *Before I scream.* "I have to catch a train. I don't want to be late meeting Jill—"

"Of course, honey, I understand." Lydia's voice dripped treacle. "I wouldn't delay you for anything. Listen, Vernon and I will come over and see you this evening."

"Oh, but—"

"Now you go and have a good time. And remember, I don't want you to worry about *anything*!"

"But—"

There was a click and the dial tone buzzed in her ear. Slowly she replaced her own receiver, staring blankly into space as though John might materialize there before her eyes, smiling and solid—and with an explanation for his conduct.

Nothing happened. The blank space in front of the door leading to the conservatory, which had been remodelled into a studio for her, remained a blank space. Behind her, the french windows opening on to the lawn let in the pale grey light of a morning advancing towards an afternoon during which no sun could be expected to shine.

Wednesday afternoon.

Which meant that John Warden Randolph, General Manager of Harding Handicrafts, was three days overdue returning from what had been scheduled as a weekend business trip to Brussels.

He had never done such a thing before without telephoning or writing to say that his plans had changed. Which meant that, here in England, he had left a series of broken appointments with colleagues and business associates scheduled from Monday morning onwards. Without apology, without explanation.

He had, it appeared, simply checked out of his Brussels hotel at noontime on Sunday, ostensibly on his way to the airport for his flight to London, and disappeared.

Oh yes. His secretary, who had accompanied him on the business trip, was also missing.

CHAPTER 2

HARVEY Livingston was the next to telephone.

Karen had just turned her blank gaze on the telephone, wondering in a vague way if she should try calling Jill Derwent to attempt to make an honest woman of herself in the unlikely event that Jill had nothing planned for this afternoon and might be available for a matinee—any matinee. Anything was better than just sitting here and—

She snatched up the telephone on the first ring. Harvey—she recognized his voice instantly—sounded taken aback.

"Karen, you were sitting right there, weren't you? On top of the phone. Waiting . . ."

"Actually," she lied briskly, "I was just passing by. I—I've been working in the garden and just decided it was time to break for an early lunch."

"That's right," he said. "Keep busy, that's the right attitude."

"Harvey—" She was obscurely grateful to him for the

stiffening he was putting into her backbone. At the best of times, he was a pompous ass. Right now—while trying to be heartening—he was insufferable. "Just what is it you want? I'm very busy right now."

"Oh yes. Yes, of course, you must be. Don't worry, it's nothing important—"

Such a disclaimer immediately roused her suspicions. "Then what is it?"

"It's—It's silly, really—"

The more he gibbered, the sharper her suspicions grew. "You might as well tell me, Harvey. It's only a question of time until I find out anyway, isn't it?"

"Well, yes. Yes, I suppose it is . . ." He trailed off unhappily.

She didn't speak again, allowing the silence to lengthen until Harvey had reached his breaking point.

"It's silly," he said again, unhappier than ever. "But—"

"I'm going out, Harvey." She nudged him gently. "Perhaps you'd like to discuss it with me later."

"No, no," he said. "There's nothing to discuss. Not with you. Probably not with John. It's just—" He sighed deeply.

She waited.

"You know, don't you—and, Karen, I don't want you to misconstrue this in any way—You know we've got the auditors in?"

"Yes." She had forgotten. She had known they were due, but then John had failed to come home and nothing else had seemed important.

"They arrived Monday," Harvey said. "They were due to come on Monday, and on Monday they arrived. They'll be here for two or three weeks—just like every year—going over the books.''

"That's usually what auditors do," she said coldly, trying to keep her voice steady. The auditors had had no relevance for her, but now she began to follow Harvey's line of thinking. How many others were thinking the same way?

"It's a coincidence, of course," Harvey went on. "Just one of those things that happen sometimes. I'm sure there's a reasonable explanation—"

"For what?" She cut him short.

"It's a question for John, really. You couldn't be expected to know the answer—" His voice lifted hopefully. "I just thought . . . possibly . . . He might have discussed it with you, and you might be able to help us out—?"

"Discussed what?"

"Well . . . the bank . . ." Harvey edged up to a reluctant point. "In the company safe deposit box at the bank . . . there were some bonds—bearer bonds. They were part of the old Harding Handicrafts assets . . . They aren't there now."

"No, Harvey," she said firmly. "I don't know anything about them." Outside the french windows the landscape dipped, wavered and blurred, threatening to disappear into a black gulf. "And I'm sure John doesn't either."

"Oh no, no," Harvey agreed quickly. "It was just that— Well, naturally, John had access—"

"Harvey, if you—"

"No, no," he placated. "Nothing like that. I'm sure there's a perfectly reasonable explanation. John probably just moved them somewhere else and was going to tell us but, before he could, he—he—" Unable to finish the sentence, Harvey floundered to a halt.

Harvey always expected other people to provide "reasonable explanations," Karen thought wryly. He was at a loss when called upon to provide one himself.

"John will be back soon," Harvey said. "Any minute now, I wouldn't be surprised—" His voice grew stronger. With the true salesman's ability to believe his own utterances, which had lifted him from a travelling position to Sales Director of the company, he was convincing himself. "This will all turn out to be a tempest in a teapot. When we find out the simple truth—and believe me, Karen, the truth is always more simple than you'd think—we'll laugh like crazy. We'll—"

"Harvey—" It seemed like ages since she had laughed at anything. She could not, at this moment, visualize herself ever laughing again. "Harvey—how much?"

"What?" She could almost hear the bump with which he descended from his rosy cloud. "What did you say?"

"I said, 'How much?'" She spelled it out for him. "How much were those bearer bonds worth?"

"Now, Karen, you don't want to take all this so seriously. It's just—"

"How much?"

His unhappiness was a palpable thing in the silence. He never could bear to tell people anything he knew they didn't want to hear. It was one of the things that had made him such a good salesman. In the circumstances, it was a giveaway trait.

"How much?"

He sighed deeply and brought himself to admit it. "A quarter of a million pounds."

CHAPTER 3

A STATE of shock, she thought. *I'm in a state of shock.*

Acting on a barely remembered principle, she put six spoonfuls of sugar into her coffee. It was then undrinkable. Tasting it, she grimaced, crossed to the sink and poured it down the drain. There must be an easier method of taking plenty of sugar.

She went to the drinks cabinet and poured a claret glass full of Tia Maria. That ought to provide ample sugar—and perhaps there might be enough caffeine content to help as well.

She sat in the wing chair beside the unlit fire and leaned back so that the protective shadows of the wings hid her face. Not that there was anyone to watch her face at the moment, but it was only a question of time until—

Her hands were shaking. Ice cold and shaking. She noted the facts with detachment. They bore little relevance to the problems of the moment and she could not afford to waste

9

any time worrying about them. She had too much thinking to do otherwise.

She took another sip of the liqueur, ignoring the way the glass in her unsteady hand clattered against her teeth. Today was Wednesday—

The telephone rang again. She pushed her head forward, like a turtle peeping from its shell, but did not move to answer it. Something in her knew that it would not be John. There was no one else she wished to talk to. She pulled her head back, leaning into the shadows of the sheltering chair. After a while, the phone stopped ringing.

Wednesday. So soon.

Sunday night had passed almost unnoticed. She had been working in her studio with a transistor radio for background music. No programmes had been interrupted with any special announcements. The usual news broadcasts had been unexciting with no mention of planes crashing—therefore, there had seemed nothing to worry about. What other threat to her happiness could there be?

As Chief Designer of the Pottery Division of Harding Handicrafts, she had no time to worry about things that might never happen. She had too much work to do. A contract had recently been negotiated with a chain of exclusive American department stores for a limited edition of a children's tea-set in a fairy-tale motif. Her proposed sketches had been admired and agreed, and now it was a question of sculpting the actual pieces.

Also, John's birthday was coming up and she was making a ceramic chess set for him. She had taken advantage of his absence to get on with that, luxuriating in the chance to work out her ideas in peace, without the necessity to stop abruptly and hide the work in progress as John's step sounded outside the studio door. It was to be a surprise for him. Furthermore, she had determined that—to the best of her ability—she would prevent Lydia and Vernon Vandergreit from ever seeing it. It was to be an original, one-off, for John alone. If Lydia and Vernon got their greedy eyes and hands on it, they would want endless reproductions for their ever-hungry American markets.

It still rankled that, in the early days of their friendship, she had designed a special flower vase for Lydia's birthday—only to find orders for its immediate incorporation into the production line. The fact that Lydia was delighted just the same was not quite the point. But she had since learned that Lydia and Vernon recognized no artistic points, registering them only as "temperament"—mysterious, inexplicable, and to be endured with humouring patience.

From then on, they were never allowed to see any originals she had thrown for personal presentations to friends. She had the uneasy feeling that, if they suspected this, they would try to do something about it.

Meanwhile, she had worked steadily through the quiet weekend, feeling only gratitude that she had been undisturbed.

Monday morning. Still no occasion for alarm. This had happened before. Especially since Harding Handicrafts had been taken over by the Brussels-based American giant. Meetings stretched out to hours beyond their projected end as what had been intended as light remarks were examined in depth . . . reservations were cancelled . . . last-minute rearrangements were made without there being time to notify anyone except those most immediately concerned.

It would not be the first time John had been delayed for impromptu conferences with executives en route from a Stateside company to a foreign subsidiary and pausing to snatch a "meaningful exchange" with European colleagues along the way. Such sessions often lasted—or were spun out—until it was time for the visiting executive to leave for the airport, at which time he graciously gave the others permission to resume their normal routines.

At times like these, John flew back on Monday morning and reported straight to the office, not arriving home until the end of the working day—or sometimes later.

But Monday night he had not come home.

Even then, it had not occurred to her to worry particularly. The postal service was indulging in one of its periodic go-slows and it was always difficult to phone through from the Continent during the height of the tourist season. Her work had gone well and she had been, in fact, still rather grateful not to be disturbed. She had worked into the early hours and then slept on the divan in the studio, as she often did when working late. She had not surfaced again until—

Tuesday afternoon.

John had not come home in the meantime, she realized, because there was no sign of his presence. Not that she expected his bed to have been slept in, but there might have been a suitcase just inside the front door, deposited there on his way to the office from the airport. He might even have snatched time to unpack a few things and shave. Obviously, he had not.

Not even a postcard. But most of the post was dated several days ago. She read it over a leisurely brunch and then decided to phone his office before going back to the studio and resuming work.

There had been a faint flurry of consternation at the switchboard when she asked to be put through to John's office after she had received no answer on his private line. She had been asked to hold on and it had been some time before a connection was finally made.

"Good afternoon, Kaa-ren. You are well, I hope?"

"Yes, thank you, Simone. And you?" It was tiresome, but these exchanges with the transplanted Continental employees had to go through a sort of conversation-book preliminary before one could get down to business. She resigned herself to a Berlitz-Baedeker interlude, one corner of her mind wondering why switchboard had connected her with the Chief Accountant, when John was so probably elsewhere—if in the building at all.

"Kaa-ren—" To her surprise, it was Simone who cut through the formalities imposed by her own Continental training. "Kaa-ren, we have been intending to call you if you have not telephoned us. Tell me, how is John? Is he feeling more well?"

"Well?" Sudden concern tightened her throat. "What's wrong with him? I thought he was at the office. You mean you've sent him home?" She saw John abruptly, vividly: running a fever; someone—Vernon, probably—insisting that John go home and go to bed; John, thinking he was stronger than he was, getting into his car and starting for home—

"No, no," Simone said. "*You* have kept him home. He has come back from Brussels ill and you have not let him come back to work. This is proper, but it is more better if

13

you telephone us and let us know when we may expect to see him again." Simone's voice took on a shading of complaint. "I must make the arrangements for the sick leave."

"But—" Something dark and malevolent fluttered at the edges of her consciousness. "John hasn't come home. He must have reported straight to the office. You must have—"

"But no," Simone interrupted. "Kaa-ren, you are not understanding me. You must concentrate, even though you *are* the *artiste*. John is with you. You must tell me how many days you are expecting this illness to last. Your National Health will be wanting documents from me—"

"No," Karen said frantically. Neither of them was understanding the other. "Simone, you don't—"

"The doctor's certificate," Simone said firmly. "This doctor's certificate, I must have. And then John can at his leisure recover. But the rules state—"

"Simone," Karen said, "Simone, John isn't—"

"This is not like you to be so obstructive, Kaa-ren," Simone complained. "We do not mind that John must lie at home, but we must have the certificate. It will not take you a moment to telephone the doctor and see that he—"

"Simone, I have not seen John! Not since Friday morning! To the best of my knowledge, he is still in Brussels. Either there, or at Harding Handicrafts. He has *not* come home!"

"This is so?" Simone's voice rose incredulously. "But Kaa-ren, how can it be? You are not make the joke?"

"I never felt less like laughing in my life," Karen assured her truthfully.

"Ooh." Simone retreated into baffled silence while she apparently tried to work out the implications of what she had just learned.

"John, then, is still in Brussels?" she asked dubiously.

"He must be. I haven't seen him since Friday. Something must have come up suddenly. I thought you'd know—"

"I will find out." Simone was suddenly crisp and businesslike at the prospect of something definite she could do. "I will telephone to Brussels Office and find out why he has not returned. I will then let you know."

"That's very kind of you," Karen said weakly. She would have preferred to telephone Brussels herself, but experience had taught everyone at the old Harding Handicrafts that once Simone got the bit between her teeth it was easier to let her gallop ahead rather than try to rein her in.

Even then, Karen had had to smile at the unconscious simile, remembering an earlier conversation with John about Simone. "She just missed being one of Henry VIII's flat-faced Flanders mares," she had remarked cattily. John had assumed a thoughtful look and trumped her, "Oh, I wouldn't say *missed*." They had both laughed then, not altogether unkindly. Despite her looks, Simone had somehow snagged one of the handsomest Englishmen heretofore out of captivity. If he were the beauty of the family and she were the brains, what did it really matter? They undoubtedly suited each other well enough. Certainly, Derek Conway seemed quite as complacent as Simone about his own abilities and his marital luck. There was no denying that he was one of the best salesmen Harding Handicrafts had every employed. And Simone's legerdemain with the ledgers was . . . well, legendary. She had risen, in a very short time, to be Chief Accountant and a Director, solely on her own merits. Harvey Livingston had often pointed out at Board Meetings just how lucky they were to have two such fine and genuine people working on their behalves.

"I will do this now," Simone said, rounding off the conversation, letting her know that it was time she hung up and allowed the businesswomen of the world to get on with their work.

"All right," Karen said. Then, feeling that something more was needed in order not to sound too cold, "Thank you, Simone. I—I really do appreciate it."

"You will be very welcome," Simone said serenely and rang off . . .

Karen spent the afternoon in her studio, immersing herself in the problem of a Magic Carpet Tazza. She had already succeeded in moulding a carpet which gave an actual impression of flight, the question now was the sort of base it should have. Should it be suspended in flight on the spire of a minaret—in which case an inner strengthening, probably a metal spike, might be needed to support it? Or should it, more prosaically, but also more economically, be resting on a base of fleecy cloud?

There was something to be said for each idea and the only way to decide was to try them both and see how they looked when fully worked out. She threw a lump of clay on to her potters' wheel and set it spinning . . .

Immersed in her work, she was momentarily startled by the sharp summons of the telephone. Then memory rushed back and she wiped her hands hurriedly and dashed for the phone.

"Kaa-ren, I have been speaking to the most stupid people," Simone complained. "They know nothing. And so I can tell you nothing." She paused. "John is not home yet?" she enquired hopefully.

"No." The disquiet which had been nibbling at her earlier now grew genuine fangs and settled down to gnaw in earnest. "No, he isn't."

"This is not to worry," Simone said firmly. "There are many other people I must call. The left hand does not know where the right hand is. I will find out."

"There might have been an accident," Karen said faintly. "Simone—have you tried the hospitals?"

"I do not think an accident." Now Simone sounded rather faint and as though some of her assurance had slipped away. "John always carries identification. You would have heard, or the Brussels Office would have been notified."

"I suppose that's true," Karen said. "But perhaps—"

"No-o-o," Simone said. An elusive note had come into her voice. "This is quite possibly nothing serious. You must not draw attention to it. Men are different and this happens sometimes. It is just—just a—"

"Simone, what are you talking about?" Sudden suspicion sharpened Karen's voice. "I don't understand you."

"This I do not understand myself." Simone's voice was silken with sympathy. "But how can we? We are women and—to us—Grace is a nothing. She is not even pretty."

"Grace? Are you talking about Grace Stevens?" John's loyal secretary of long and devoted service—what had she to do with this?

"Of course, Grace. You do not know?" Despite the sympathy, a note of bland relish crept into Simone's voice. "Grace has not come back to the office either. And I cannot reach her at her flat. She is not there. And John is not with you.

17

"I understand how you will feel, Kaa-ren, but you must be brave. And you must do nothing to draw attention to this state of affairs—"

"This is absurd," Karen broke in. "Simone, you're mad to even think of such a thing!"

"Naturally, you feel this way," Simone purred. "I have, in the past, felt this way myself. But you must realize, Kaaren—" her voice took on the crisp note of a Chief Accountant—"two and two make—"

Karen hung up abruptly.

CHAPTER 4

WEDNESDAY. And the vultures were gathering.
Oh, very discreetly, of course. Nothing so
blatant as perching on the tree branches outside
waiting for the death-rattle before closing in.

No, it was more of a wheeling through the sky above the
devastated area, in ever-decreasing circles, hovering, waiting to drop on their prey when it was at its weakest and
unable to resist.

The telephone and the doorbell both began to ring at
once. Neither of them raised any false hopes in her, especially not the doorbell. John had his own key.

She remained absolutely quiet, her breathing shallow, as
though by the very quality of her stillness she could convince them that the house was empty, so that they would go
away and not bother her.

At first she thought it was working. The telephone kept
ringing, but the doorbell stopped. Then she heard the sound
of footsteps on the gravel path. Whoever it was had decided to

come round to the side and try to get in through the french windows which were usually unlocked and frequently, in weather as good as this, ajar.

She couldn't be caught huddling here like a wounded animal. And there was only one acceptable excuse for not answering the door—

"Hello?" She caught up the phone, hoping that the person on the other end would have hung up. She could then stand murmuring meaningless phrases into the receiver and appear perfectly legitimate to anyone looking in from outside without actually having to think.

"Karen, you *are* there! I've caught you in time." Jill Derwent's voice, lively with concern, thrummed across the wires. "What on earth is going on?"

"Going on?" Karen sipped at her drink, watching as Lydia hove into view.

"Karen, don't play word games with *me*." Her cousin's voice took on a warning note. "I know you too well. And besides, a little bird has been telling tales out of school."

"Bird?" Karen's attention was fully occupied by Lydia and the way she was behaving beyond the french windows.

Oddly, she had made no attempt to approach the house. Instead, she had pussyfooted over to the empty garage and was peering through its windows. Even as Karen watched, she scrubbed at a window with her handkerchief and then leaned against it, shielding her eyes with her hands, the better to see inside.

"A little Southern bird," Jill elaborated. "With honeysuckle and magnolia blossoms falling from her beak. But tactful—so tactful I couldn't figure out what the hell she was talking about—"

"I see," Karen said vaguely. What she actually saw was Lydia turning to survey the house thoughtfully before starting to move purposefully towards the french windows.

"That's more than *I* can say," Jill said tartly. "Karen, what *is* going on? I could only gather that you were in desperate trouble but, despite that, you were on your way to London to go to that matinee with me—and I was to be very kind and understanding towards you."

"Yes, that's right," Karen said. Lydia had just sighted her through the french windows and stepped up her advance, waving wildly all the way.

"You're not alone?" Thank heaven for Jill's ability to sum up a situation quickly. "You can't talk. Just answer 'yes' or 'no'—shall I come down?"

"Yoo-hoo, yoo-hoo—" Lydia was swinging open the french windows, yodelling like a Swiss mountaineer on the rampage, apparently under the impression that she was invisible when not audible. "Yoo-hoo, Karen. Here I am!"

"No, please," Karen said urgently into the telephone. "No, don't. Everything is all right." She slammed down the receiver and turned to Lydia with a frozen smile.

"There now," Lydia said. "I just had a little bet with myself that I'd find you on the telephone and that was why you couldn't answer the door." A flick of her eyes, a faint assessing sniff, and then she averted her gaze from the glass in Karen's hand.

"It rang for a while before I heard it," Karen said. What a fascinating story Lydia would have to tell the Board Members of the parent company some day—all about the absconding General Manager of their English subsidiary and his dipsomaniac wife. "I was working in the studio."

"Off in one of your artistic trances," Lydia said, "*I* know. May I just peek and—" She began tiptoeing towards the studio as though it were a nursery containing sleeping infants.

"I'd rather you didn't," Karen said.

Lydia stopped short and turned a hurt look upon her.

"It's rather a mess in there, I'm afraid."

"Oh, I don't mind that." She should never have tried to give a polite excuse. Lydia started for the studio again. "I guess I've seen as bad a mess as ever you could make in any time. I never let a little thing like that bother me."

"I'm sorry." Unable to remember whether she had tossed a cloth over the chess set to protect it from prying eyes, Karen moved swiftly, blocking Lydia's way. "I really can't let anyone see it in that state." She smiled, falling back on the one line Lydia would not be able to refute. "Put it down to my artistic temperament."

"Oh, you artists!" Lydia said, but something dangerous flashed deep in her eyes. "What *can* the rest of us do with you?"

"Sit down, Lydia." Karen shamelessly crowded her backwards until she lost her balance and fell into the arms of the wing chair. "Can I get you a drink?"

"Not at this—" Lydia broke off with an embarrassed laugh. "Well, I guess the sun *is* over the yardarm, as you folks say. Just a teensy-weensy one, then."

Karen recklessly splashed gin into a glass, ignoring Lydia's wincing protest. "Where's Vernon? I thought he was coming with you."

"Oh, not *now*." Lydia took the glass dubiously. "No, Vernon's at the office. There are so many things to see to—"

She broke off, obviously abruptly aware of her *faux pas* and smiled at Karen uneasily.

"I—to tell the truth—" She smiled nervously again. "I was going to be all on my lonesome this afternoon, and I got to thinking about what you said about going up to London for a matinee. And I thought to myself, "Why, that sounds like great fun," and so I thought maybe I could horn in. I mean, I've got the car and I thought I could drive you up—and there's almost always an extra seat going at the box office. Just for one, it isn't difficult. Of course, we wouldn't be sitting together, but that wouldn't matter. And then we could drive back together, and it would be so much nicer for you than the dreary old train—"

"I see," Karen said slowly. "That was really very thoughtful of you, Lydia."

It must have been a long time since Lydia had blushed, and she didn't now. "On second thought—" Lydia daintily set her drink on the coffee table beside her chair—"this probably isn't a good idea. I'll be driving."

"I'm sorry, I forgot to tell you." Karen watched Lydia carefully as she cut the ground from under her. "My plans have changed. I won't be going to London this afternoon, after all. But don't let me spoil your day," she added blandly. "You go right ahead."

"Oh, I couldn't go without you," Lydia said quickly. "I mean—" Karen watched the bemused expression spread across her face as she struggled to paraphrase what she *did* mean.

"Oh, but you must," Karen insisted. "I couldn't forgive myself if I thought I'd ruined your outing."

"But, honey, you were the cause of it—" Lydia floundered in deeper. "I mean—I mean, I just couldn't leave you here alone."

And you didn't want to leave me alone in London, either. Karen took a sip of her drink, lest she say the words aloud. It was awkward enough to have a jailer without pointing up the situation and making it even more awkward for both of them.

"The weather's too nice to be stuck in an old theatre in the city, anyway," Lydia said, ignoring any vibrations from unspoken words in the air. "Why don't you go out in the garden and sit in the chaise-longue and I'll put a kettle on and find something we can have for lunch?"

Why not? If their positions had been reversed, if it had been Vernon who had disappeared, and John who would have to answer to the Board of Directors, wouldn't she have been the one to rally round—and keep an eye on Lydia to make sure that she didn't slip away and join her errant husband?

Ah, but Lydia's husband didn't *have* a secretary. Vernon simply sent for the first girl available from the secretarial pool when he had letters to dictate, or errands to be run. Wise Vernon. Or was it wise Lydia, who had instigated such a programme so long ago that Vernon had come to think of it as his own idea?

"Come on." Lydia's hand was on her arm, urging her towards the french windows. "You just stretch out in the sun and try to get some rest. I'll bet you didn't sleep much last night, did you?"

"Actually, I took a sleeping pill."

"Now that was downright sensible of you! I think you're taking this just the right way. It's all some kind of mix-up and you don't want to get all hot and bothered about it. Not that I could ever imagine you getting hot and bothered for one teensy-weensy minute.''

She could do without Lydia's applause. Karen sank down on the chaise-longue and managed to escape the guiding hand.

"Here now—'' Lydia began plumping up cushions. "Isn't this better? You've been working too hard anyway, honey. You just ought to relax for a few days, and maybe we could have Dr. Feltham come over later this afternoon and give you a few tranquilizers—just to get you through the next few days until—''

Until we find out the truth? And perhaps after we find out—when you may need them even more.

Karen looked up unexpectedly and caught the expression on Lydia's face.

Although her voice was brimming with warm concern, Lydia's eyes were cold and assessing as she stared at the glass in Karen's hand and then seemed to dismiss the idea of relieving her of it as perhaps too pointed at this stage. She gave a faint negative shake of her head, as though silently reproving herself, and an even fainter sigh, then seemed to become aware of Karen's eyes on her face.

"There—'' The bright mechanical smile was back on her face instantly. "You'll be more comfortable now. You just lean back and don't you worry about a *thing*—''

There was obviously going to be only one way to get rid of Lydia. Karen leaned back and closed her eyes firmly.

"That's right—'' Despite the fact that her instructions were being obeyed, Lydia sounded slightly at a loss. "You rest . . . Unless it would help you to talk about it a little—?''

Resisting the temptation to peep at Lydia's face, Karen shook her head.

"Of course, it's up to you. I wouldn't want to disturb you for one little minute, but sometimes people feel better if they can talk to a sympathetic ear. Let it all pour out—"

If I knew, do you think I'd tell you? Karen's lips tightened, she shook her head again.

"Of course, I realize there's probably nothing to tell." Lydia began backtracking hastily. "I just thought—"

Not even Lydia could keep talking to an obdurate shuttered face. "Well, never mind what I thought. You know how silly I can be sometimes. You rest and I'll go and put the kettle on now."

When Karen opened her eyes, Lydia was retreating across the lawn.

CHAPTER 5

LYDIA was barely out of sight behind the french windows when Karen remembered that the studio door was unlocked. She struggled upright, spilling a bit of her drink in the awkward process. For an arrested moment, she watched the dark brown splash seeping slowly into the dark brown earth between the blades of grass, then thoughtfully tilted her glass to pour out the rest of the drink.

Libation to the gods. What ridiculous notions could surface from the depths of some primitive layer of superstition in one's subconscious. *No gods could help her now.*

Carrying the empty glass, she moved across the lawn, avoiding the gravel path, approaching the french windows soundlessly from the grass. The windows were ajar and Lydia had her back to them, speaking into the telephone.

"—it isn't there." There was a pause while the person on the other end of the line evidently asked a question or gave some instruction.

"I intend to," Lydia said decisively. "I'm not at all sure—"

Karen must have made some faint sound, or perhaps a shadow on the wall betrayed her. At any rate, Lydia was suddenly aware that someone was behind her and turned around abruptly.

"What are—?" Lydia focused on Karen's face, then she took a deep breath and began again.

"Why, honey, I thought you were going to lie in the sun and rest for a while."

"I brought the glass back." Karen held it out apologetically, as though this were Lydia's home and she were the intrusive guest.

"You needn't have done that." Lydia did not seem to notice that she had been holding the telephone. Her earlier remark had been spoken over the mouthpiece and now, in a smooth casual movement, she replaced the receiver without having said anything more to the other person—not even goodbye.

"You could have put it down beside the chaise-longue— or even called me and I'd have come and taken it." Lydia moved kitchenwards, away from the telephone. As though she had not been using it at all. Or hoped that Karen would not notice that she had been.

"I wanted a sweater," Karen said smoothly. "It's cooler outside than it looks." Perhaps they were right to distrust her when she could lie so easily. Even she had not suspected this capability within herself.

"It usually is—in this country." Lydia accepted the explanation without surprise. "You just sit down there and tell me which sweater you want and I'll run up and get it for you quicker than quick."

"That won't be necessary." Even through the cotton-wool layers of shock that cocooned her off from the world, this bland assumption of Lydia's that she had been deprived of all physical facilities was becoming irritating. "I know just what I want and where it is. I can get it far more quickly than you can."

As though time mattered. As though time had not stopped on . . . Sunday? Or Monday? Or Tuesday . . . When?

"Well—" Lydia looked dubious. "If you're absolutely sure—"

"Isn't that the kettle I hear?" Karen lifted her head questioningly.

"Oh, er—it might be." Lydia was temporarily stalemated. To admit that she had not yet put the kettle on might lead to questions about what she *had* been doing. Second and third thoughts seemed to flash across her face, ending with a decision to retreat as gracefully as possible. "I'll just go and see."

Karen waited until she heard the sound of water surreptitiously gushing into the kettle from the tap before she moved. Then she crossed silently to the studio door, opened it, reached around it and removed the key from the inside lock, transferred it swiftly to her side of the door, closed the door and turned the key. The gush of relief she felt at having accomplished this told her that she had been under greater tension than she had realized.

Holding the key tightly in her hand, she ascended the stairs. A sweater—perhaps a cardigan—with pockets, that was what she wanted now, so that she could keep the key with her.

The bedroom seemed dark and enormous, the big double bed looked wide enough to engulf several people. Even the mirror seemed darker, as though the silver had tarnished overnight. It all seemed suspended in a curious vacuum.

She crossed to the wardrobe and pulled out a thick-knit oatmeal jacket with large patch pockets. Their Unisex jacket, John had called it. Big enough to fit either of them, and with a loose tie-belt and no buttons. They were in the habit of using it interchangeably when either of them just wanted to sit outdoors, or go for a short jaunt in the car.

Karen put it on, finding a faint comfort in the familiar folds, and thrust her hands into the pockets, opening one hand to allow the studio key to fall loose into a corner.

There were already keys there. She pulled them out and looked at them blankly for a moment before recognition came. Of course, they were John's spare set of car keys. He had been wearing the jacket last weekend when he drove to the local garage to have some minor adjustment made to the steering and the petrol tank filled. She dropped them back into the pocket. Like the studio key, she would know where they were when needed. Right now, the car would be at the airport parking lot, waiting for John to reclaim it when he returned from—

She switched her mind away from that thought and crossed over to the dressing-table, taking a few paper handkerchiefs from the dispenser to cram into her pocket to muffle the jangle of metal when she moved. There was no point in calling Lydia's attention to the whereabouts of any keys.

"Honey, are you all right—?" As though thinking about her had conjured her up, Lydia stood in the doorway, peering at Karen.

Why shouldn't I be? Once again, she tried to restrain her

sense of irritation. It was not Lydia's fault that they were both in this position. *But it wasn't her fault either.*

"Of course." She picked up a lipstick and leaned forward into the mirror, automatically running the tube of colour over her lips. It was a shade that John hated, she realized too late, but that didn't matter now. *Perhaps it would never matter again.*

She replaced the lipstick and took up a perfume phial, splashing the scent recklessly on to throat and wrists. John knew she was nearly out of it and was going to bring back a fresh dutyfree—

"I'm just coming." Shaken at the way her mind could still betray her, she put down the perfume and turned blankly from the mirror. She *knew*—it was seared into her mind as nothing else had ever been before, as perhaps nothing would ever be again—*knew* that John had disappeared, might not *be* coming home. And yet, from some corner of her consciousness, could come the smooth assurance that nothing had changed; nothing more serious than a flight delay had occurred, and that everything would be going on as before.

"It will be better downstairs." Lydia reached out sympathetically, as though she would put an arm around her waist, and then drew back almost shyly. "Come on."

"Yes, downstairs," Karen said. She paused in the doorway, looking back into the empty echoing room. She knew suddenly that she would not sleep there again. Not until John came home.

Until then, she would sleep in the studio, where she could feel warmer, safer. On the very comfortable divan bed in the studio, surrounded—and supported—by her work in progress all around her.

31

"That's right, honey." She was aware, as from a distance, that Lydia was leading her, coaxing her, down the stairs, into the living-room, and pushing her gently, seating her in the big wing chair.

"Would you rather have tea or coffee, honey? It's no trouble, whichever you want. I could do with a cup myself." Lydia carefully refrained from specifying which, presumably in order not to sway her choice.

"Poor Lydia." Karen looked at her suddenly, noting the lines of strain across her forehead and around her eyes. "You and Vernon *do* have your problems with your foreign colleagues, don't you?"

"Now, honey, I don't want to hear you talking that way." Lydia's eyes narrowed slightly, losing something of their sympathetic glint. "You aren't a colleague—you're a friend. And your problems are my problems."

Not quite. Vernon would be coming home tonight. And Vernon was in the country—available for consultation—now. Karen was abruptly certain that it was Vernon to whom Lydia had been speaking during that interrupted telephone conversation. It had all been done too smoothly, bespeaking too much practice. She would not dare to treat anyone else in that manner. Only her husband—only Vernon.

"I'd like tea, please." She smiled sweetly at Lydia. That would keep Lydia out of the way longer than coffee. Tea was still fairly new territory to Lydia and she would take more time trying to find all the proper equipment and trying to brew it properly.

"In two shakes of a lamb's tail," Lydia said cheerfully, and highly inaccurately. She whisked away as though she were as happy to go as Karen was to see her go.

Karen leaned back into the wing chair and closed her eyes. When she opened them again—*if* she opened them again—it might be to the day before yesterday, to last week, to the world as it used to be, to—

The telephone shrilled abruptly. She did not move, did not open her eyes, knowing that the miracle had not—could not have—happened. The telephone went on ringing.

"Hello?" Lydia had come in from the kitchen, footsteps sounding briskly, even on the carpet, to answer.

"Oh, Simone. No—no, it's me, Lydia. She's asleep. I don't want to wake her. She's had enough—"

Simone evidently cut in with some remark. Karen kept her eyes closed and could hear annoyance in Lydia's tone.

"No, you can't talk to her right now. There can't be anything so important that it can't wait for a little while longer—"

Again a silence while something was protested at the other end of the line.

"Is there any message, Simone?" Lydia asked dismissively. "If not, I'll tell her you called."

The sound of the receiver crashing down was audible even from where Karen sat. Then came the more controlled, reserved click of Lydia's receiver being replaced.

"Well," she said thoughtfully to Karen's inert form. "I didn't think you'd feel like talking to *her* right now."

Without waiting for a reply, she returned to the kitchen, leaving Karen unsure as to whether Lydia had seen through her slight deception, or just spoken her thoughts as a matter of course.

CHAPTER 6

"NOW, we must not panic." Harvey Livingston ran his handkerchief over his forehead, not for the first time. "This is a time when we must have faith in each other, when we must stand firm." He tugged at his already loosened tie, and undid the top button of his shirt.

"I reiterate—" He glared at them as though he had been challenged. "We must not panic."

"But, Har-vee," Simone said, in tones of sweet reasonableness. "It is not to panic. Kaa-ren only asks whether we have notified the police yet." She hesitated. "This is the question, surely, that any wife would ask."

That any innocent party would ask, she meant.

"Of course, of course," Harvey said. "I am not disputing that, Simone. I am simply pointing out that we must not take precipitate action at this point. It could do more harm than good."

Wednesday night—seventy-two hours. Scarcely precipitate. The police might wonder why they had not been notified well before this point—in view of all the circumstances.

"But, Har-vee—" Simone had obviously had the same thought—"if we do not mention this to the police soon, will they not be annoyed when we do?"

"I can't see how they would be," Harvey shot Simone a harassed look. "They ought to be the first to understand that we would want to allow a trusted colleague time to—" He avoided Karen's eyes. "Time to come to his senses."

Lydia made a little tut-tutting sound of distress. She turned to Karen.

"Honey, are you sure you want to stay here and listen to all this? It isn't going to do you any good. Why don't you go upstairs and lie down—?"

Not upstairs. "I'm all right," Karen said. Furthermore, she was vitally concerned. More so than any of them. How could they imagine that she might docilely retire to a darkened chamber and allow them to sort out her fate? "I'll stay."

"After all—" Harvey was in full flight. "This is John Warden Randolph we're talking about. *Our* John—not some fly-by-night Johnny-come-lately who wormed his way into a position of responsibility. We thought—*think*—the world of John. He kept Harding Handicrafts afloat during dark stormy times, he steered it through financial reefs and into the safe harbour of Vendergreit Enterprises. We were proud and pleased to give him a seat on our Board of Directors—"

At Simone's side, Derek Conway stirred restlessly. Apart from Karen, he was the only person in the room who was not on the Board of Directors. One always suspected that it rankled.

"We cannot withdraw our faith in him at this time. Why—" Harvey's tone broadened into forced jocularity— "why, to suspect John would be as unthinkable as suspecting Vernon, here!"

Vernon tried to look modest and succeeded in looking sanctimonious. "Hear, hear," Lydia murmured, patting his hand.

"Men have brainstorms." Simone shrugged. "This is well known."

Everyone carefully refrained from glancing at Derek, one of whose brainstorms had left the typing pool and subsequently given birth to twins in London four months later. It was another reason why he would never be offered that coveted seat on the Board of Directors. The wise executive doesn't foul his own nest.

"Well, I agree with Karen." Lydia was sitting between Karen and Vernon. This time she leaned over and patted Karen's hand. "I think you're just jumping to the worst possible conclusion without any real evidence at all."

The worst possible conclusion? That was an interesting sidelight on Lydia's own character. Did she honestly believe that it was worse for a man to disappear for a—a *fling* with his secretary than to be lying dead and unidentified in some foreign morgue? Karen preferred Simone's brainstorm theory. From a brainstorm, a man could come back. Derek was living proof of that. *Living.*

"I still think the Belgian police should be contacted," Karen said. "I'm sure your Brussels office is very good— but I believe the police would do a better job of checking all the hospitals. They'll know of places—"

"Ah yes," Harvey said. He looked like a man who was wishing he could remove his jacket but did not feel that either the occasion or the temperature really warranted such an action. "Yes, believe me, Karen, I do see your point."

"Honey, you've just got to be patient," Lydia said. "These things work themselves out in their own time. We can't—"

"Every possible enquiry has been made. And in all the correct places. I have checked this personally." Simone appeared to be affronted. "The police could not do more."

"I feel we are off on a tangent." Vernon intervened, as though calling a meeting to order. "I feel that we are making a mistake by concentrating on the negative aspect so much. We should look for something positive."

As at a Board Meeting, one by one the heads turned towards him, almost in awe. Even those who were accustomed to seeing Vernon in action could still be astounded by the heights of fatuity to which he could rise.

"But continue, Vernon." Simone's voice was carefully bland. "We are all most anxious to learn what positive aspects you have found in this."

"Now, that is why were are here," Vernon said. "So that Karen can help us. To start with, Karen—" he leaned forward earnestly. "I want you to tell us everything John said to you before he left on Friday."

"He didn't say anything." Karen tried to match his calm tone. "All he said was goodbye."

Simone nodded as though a private opinion had been confirmed.

"Now, Karen," Vernon said. "You're being negative again."

"I didn't mean that," Karen said. "I just meant he said goodbye—the way he does every time he goes off on a business trip. There was nothing different about this time."

"Are you sure?" Harvey seemed to feel that he had been out of the action long enough. "We want you to think carefully, Karen. Think very, very carefully."

"It was just like any other trip," Karen insisted. *What did they imagine? That John had kissed her passionately, murmured, "Meet me in Istanbul in a fortnight," and slipped a forged passport into her hand?*

Yes. She looked around despairingly at their intent, humourless faces. *Yes, that was probably just what they did imagine.*

Of course, that didn't account for Grace.

"Just start at the beginning," Harvey prompted. "The alarm went off and you got up—"

"We came downstairs and had breakfast." She picked up the thread dutifully, humouring them. It was the only way to prove that there was nothing useful for them to learn. "Then John said goodbye and—"

"Now, now, take it more slowly. You're skipping over things. We want—" Vernon frowned at her portentously— "we want to know about *everything*."

"But—"

"For instance," Harvey put in helpfully, "what did you have for breakfast?"

Caviar and champagne. Followed by baked stuffed peacock—

"And *who*—" Lydia nodded pointedly—"cooked it?"

They were trying to be kind. They were *kind.* Another Board of Directors might have done more than check the

38

hospitals and try to dissuade her from calling the police. With a quarter of a million pounds in bearer bonds missing, a less loyal group of colleagues might have rushed to the police without even talking to her first. The first she knew about it might have been when the newspaper reporters appeared at the door.

"Take it from the beginning again," Vernon said. "Start with getting up."

"John got up first and went into the bathroom." She must try to be co-operative. "He'd packed the night before, just leaving his case open to put in the last-minute things. Then, when he came out and packed his toothbrush and shaving kit, I went in."

"Just a minute—" Vernon said. "What were you doing in the meantime?"

"Meantime—?"

"While he was in the bathroom."

"I turned over and napped for another few minutes." There was no reason she should feel so defensive about it. "I was working late the night before. On the Fairy-tale Tea-Set," she reminded him.

"Yes, yes." He forgave her. "That's all right."

The American Directors were slightly schizophrenic where she was concerned. On the one hand, it was practically sacred writ to them that company wives should have no other reason for existence than to stand by their husbands, have meals waiting for them when they came in, listen breathlessly to every utterance—and chime in with any brilliant ideas that might help said husband climb to the top. Lydia was a shining example of this. On no account was the wife expected to have any interest outside the home. Certainly she was not expected to have a career of her own.

On the other hand, Karen was a valuable member of the creative staff. Furthermore, she had already been married to John when Harding Handicrafts had been taken over. They had been forced to swallow their prejudices and accept the situation as they found it, their desire to press her to conform to company tradition counterbalanced by their realization that they would lose one of the best designers in the ceramic field if they did. An uneasy truce had been declared, but there were moments when she could still see that it rankled.

"Go on, dear." Lydia was carefully masking her opinion of a woman who would not leap out of bed and joyously prepare her husband's breakfast.

"When I came out of the bath, John had dressed and gone downstairs. I heard him putting the kettle on." Karen speeded up her narrative. "I got dressed and went down. He was on the telephone, so I started breakfast—"

"Wait a minute, wait a minute," Vernon said. "Who was he on the telephone *to*? Do you know that?

"Why, it was Grace—" That had not occurred to her before. "Grace had called him and—"

"Did this happen often?" Vernon's voice and face were carefully expressionless. "Grace calling, I mean? And at that hour of the morning?"

"Not often, no." She tried to keep emotion out of her own voice. It didn't mean a thing. It could all be explained. "But when she was travelling with him—every seven or eight trips, perhaps—he picked her up and she drove to the airport with him. She was just calling to let him know she was ready."

"I see. So Grace was with him practically from the moment he left the house?"

"If you want to put it like that, yes. It would take him five or ten minutes to get over to her place, of course, and collect her."

"Grace has always lived nearby?" Simone slid a thoughtful look to her fellow directors.

"This isn't a very large town," Karen said coldly. "By car, I doubt if anyone lives more than ten minutes away."

"Of course, of course." Harvey glared at Simone. "We are not disputing that, Karen. Try to be more objective. We are on your side, remember."

I didn't know we were choosing sides. And, if we are, who's on John's side? He was quietly being condemned without a hearing. Every question they asked, every minute they put off calling the police, was adding to the condemnation. Worse, might be cutting off his chances of survival. If the hire car had crashed—If he and Grace were lying injured and undiscovered in some ditch or hedgerow, unconscious, unable to call for help—

Karen stood abruptly and crossed to the telephone. While they watched silently, she began to dial for the Continental Operator. If no one else would do it, she must contact the Belgian police herself, explain the situation, set them to searching every possible place—however unlikely. John must be given every chance.

"What do you think you're doing?" It was Vernon who spoke. Vernon, outraged at the sight of someone else grasping any sort of initiative when he was there.

"I'm calling Belgium." She did not bother to look at

him, already rehearsing the awkward phrases she must use to try to explain—

A slim hand slapped down the cradle, cutting off her call. She looked up angrily, but Simone was staring across the room, meeting another pair of eyes.

"It is no use, Har-vee" she said softly. "You will have to tell her. You should have told her as soon as you were sure."

"Tell me what?" Karen, too, swung to face Harvey.

"Now, now." He was earnestly, desperately placating. "Take it easy, Karen. We're only trying to do what's best for you."

"Tell her, Har-vee."

"There's no use telephoning Belgium." Harvey capitulated abruptly, swiping at his moist forehead again. "They can't do anything there."

"I think we need more of an explanation than that, Harvey." Vernon Vandergreit brought the full force of his personality to bear as Harvey hesitated.

"Yes, yes." Harvey tugged at his tie, further loosening it. "The fact is, we've spent all day checking this out. Brussels Office report that the hire car was left at the airport Sunday afternoon—just as it should have been if they were catching the usual flight. Furthermore, their reservations were confirmed, their tickets collected, their seats occupied for that flight." He paused, looking unhappier than ever.

"Continue, Har-vee." Simone pushed him inexorably.

"Yes, yes. Well, there's no doubt about it. No doubt at all. They're back in this country. Both of them."

CHAPTER 7

"**Y**OU'RE sure?" Vernon glared at him severely. "We checked this afternoon. The company car was collected from the airport parking lot just after the flight landed on Sunday."

"You didn't—?"

"No, no." Harvey was instantly defensive. "Of course not. I went up there myself. I wouldn't drag anyone else into it at this stage. The fewer who know—"

"Good thinking!" Vernon relaxed. "We don't want this to get around."

She had not felt Simone's hand under her arm, leading her back to her chair. Nor did she really attend to what was being said around her. Why should it suddenly seem less likely that John could have met with an accident here in England? People had accidents every day. There were constant pile-ups on the motorways. You had only to look at the newspapers or turn on the television—

And that was it. Accidents in this country were well

documented, recorded, reported. They were traceable, even by a layman. The chances of an undiscovered accident were so remote as to be almost impossible.

From a great distance, she heard a faint whisper and did not recognize it as her own.

"Get her some brandy," Simone ordered.

Derek leaped to obey. Dear Derek—if it weren't for his little infidelities, he would have been the perfect company wife. Certainly, Simone was of far more value to the company than he was. They could always hire another salesman. They could not find another accountant so able and devoted as Simone.

"I'm not sure that's wise." Lydia stood up, obviously attempting to warn tactfully that their missing General Manager's wife was an incipient, if not active, dipsomaniac. "Why don't I go and make us all some coffee?"

Derek hesitated, looking from Simone to Lydia, as though unsure whether his own wife or the Chairman's wife took precedence.

"Brandy!" Simone snapped, ending his dilemma. He moved unerringly to the drinks cabinet and found the bottle and glasses.

"I think coffee would be very welcome, dear." Vernon came to his wife's rescue. "I'm sure we'd all like some."

"That's right," Harvey backed him up with measured heartiness. "Coffee will be just the ticket right now." He glanced at the brandy with a faint wistfulness.

"It won't take any time at all," Lydia assured them and escaped to the kitchen.

"I, too, will have a brandy, Derek." The flash of Simone's eyes hinted at her opinion of those who would try to curry favour with the parent company by repressing their own wishes in order to fall into any line dictated by the Vandergreits. "Will you not have one as well, Derek?"

"Oh no. No, thank you." Derek removed his hand from the bottle and hastily brought over their drinks, moving away from Simone again quickly. "I'll wait for the coffee. That sounds just fine to me."

"As you wish." Simone shrugged, dismissing him, returning her attention to Karen. "Drink, Kaa-ren, it will do you good."

Nothing will do me any good. But she raised the glass to her lips and sipped at it. She felt a faint warmth, a warmth that could never hope to reach the icy fastnesses deep in her being.

She was dimly aware of eyes meeting over her head, of unspoken messages vibrating in the air around her. But none of it mattered. Except that it meant that she was surrounded by people—however well-meaning—at a time when she desperately needed to be alone to assimilate what she had learned and to try to come to terms with it.

"Now you can understand, Karen, how very important it is that you should try to remember everything that you can." Harvey frowned at her with the air of having scored a vital point.

"There's nothing to remember." She leaned back and closed her eyes, shutting out the intent anxious faces. She felt an almost overpowering need to walk into the studio, close and lock the door behind her, and sink her fingers into the soft yielding clay, letting her mind go blank.

"Perhaps Harvey phrased that badly." Vernon Vandergreit's voice beat insistently at her attention. "What we mean is, we want you to think back over the past few weeks—oh, you don't have to try all at once. But begin trying to recall anything, any little thing at all, that might have been unusual—even if it didn't seem particularly so at the time. Any little deviations from routine, any remark that was out of character, any—"

"This is very well, but Kaa-ren is exhausted." Simone was the only one of them with any sense, any human understanding. "It is time we left her to sleep. In the morning, we can telephone and ask if she has remembered anything when she is rested."

"Oh no!" Lydia, carrying in a tray with coffee and cups, cried out in sudden consternation. "No, I mean—" She deposited the tray on a table and abandoned it to argue with Simone.

"I mean, this is no time for Karen to be alone. She needs her friends around her. In fact, I'm going to send Vernon home to fetch my nightie and *I'm* going to stay here with her *all night*."

"Oh no!" The announcement snapped Karen out of her lethargy. "Thank you, Lydia, but that won't be necessary."

"Necessary!" Lydia dismissed the protest. "There's no such word as 'necessary' between friends."

"You've done quite enough." Karen tried to keep the trace of asperity out of her voice. Lydia had been here all afternoon, insisting on cooking dinner for her, following her around, making inane little observations of the blessings she still had left to count. "More than enough."

"Enough—" Lydia began.

"Cream and sugar?" Derek had taken over the neglected

coffee tray and was pouring. Simone gave him an approving nod at this timely intervention and immediately provided a further diversion herself.

"So, the company car has gone as well. We purchased it eighteen months ago—" A rapt light appeared in her eyes as she gave herself over to mental calculations. "We have had one year's depreciation on it—"

"Simone! For heaven's sake—not now!" Lydia's cry of outrage rose to a shriek. "Not in front of poor Karen!"

"That's right, Simone." Harvey looked pained. "I really feel this is neither the time nor the place."

"That is well for you to speak, Har-vee. It is not you who has to face the auditors in the morning!"

"I think I may say, without fear of contradiction—" Vernon seemed to have decided that the time was ripe to make a speech—"this is a difficult situation for all of us—"

A difficult situation. John had used those words nearly three years ago. When Harding Handicrafts had begun to sink into the slough of troubles that nearly overwhelmed it, that had certainly led to their eventually accepting the bid from Vandergreit Enterprises to take over Harding Handicrafts. And that had not been all he had said—or done—at that time. But that could not be what Vernon meant when he asked her to recall anything unusual. That had been long before Vandergreit Enterprises had appeared on the horizon. That had been another time when things had seemed pretty desperate.

"I think we'd better put the house in your name," John had said. *"That way, you'll be taken care of, whatever happens."*

Whatever happens. But he had meant the threat of bankruptcy proceedings. With so much of his capital tied up in

Harding Handicrafts, that was the worst he had in mind. It was one of the standard procedures for businessmen in difficulties, and there was no question of an attempt to default on creditors. If bankruptcy had been declared, John would have devoted years to ensuring that every creditor received 100 pence to the pound—eventually.

Not that it would have come to that. The bearer bonds alone—taken out at a time when the old Chairman had envisaged branching out on the takeover trail himself—were enough to post as surety. And there were investments, shares in other companies—although at that time, no companies were doing so well that their shares could be regarded as gilt-edged.

Whatever happens. The papers had been duly passed and she had thought no more about it. Perhaps she should have. *Grace had been his secretary then.* Was it possible that he had been planning something like this so far back as that?

If not, the fact that such legal formalities had taken place would have made it easier for him to reach such a decision when the time came.

No! She pulled her mind away, abruptly realizing the depths of treachery into which it was leading her. *There must be a reasonable explanation. An innocent explanation. Things could not be the way they looked.*

If they were, then her entire life with John had been a lie, her marriage a monstrous farce.

"Kaa-ren is unwell." Simone's voice came to her from a great distance. "This is not surprising. It is time we left her to rest."

"I agree," Lydia said. "Karen, honey, I'll go and run a nice warm tub for you. And Vernon—you go fetch my night things. I'll look after her."

Back to square one. Did Lydia never drop an idea once she got her teeth into it?

"No, please—" Karen opened her eyes, instinctively looking to Simone for help, but Simone was frowning thoughtfully.

"Perhaps it is best you are not now alone, Kaa-ren." She added with serene tactlessness, "If you prefer, *I* will remain here with you tonight."

A faint shudder of hysteria rippled over her. Did she look as though she might be going to slash her wrists as soon as the door had closed behind everyone?

Simone and Lydia had withdrawn to one side and were murmuring together earnestly. Harvey crossed the room and knelt by her chair.

"I know it looks bad . . ." He patted her hand. "But you've got to hang on . . . and we'll . . ." Looking up, he encountered Simone's sardonic eye and faltered to a stop.

We'll . . . what? Find him for you? Catch him? Bring him back—willing or not? *With or without Grace?*

And then what? Things can go on as before? Hardly likely. There are brainstorms and brainstorms. A brainstorm involving a secret weekend with a willing secretary was quite different from a brainstorm involving decamping with a quarter of a million pounds, plus the said secretary, plus the company car.

That bespoke a finality from which there was no turning back. Even if, by some unlikely miracle, John could be found, the money restored, and the whole incident hushed up, he would not be welcomed back to the Board of Directors with open arms. And would she welcome him back with open arms—after Grace?

It was a question she couldn't answer. Not now, with all of them watching her, discussing her, trying to decide what to do about her, as though she were some inanimate object requiring extensive care and treatment, but with no ability to participate in any decision regarding her ultimate destiny.

"Well then, that's settled!" Vernon's voice rose slightly, a decisive man making a decision. "Simone will stay here tonight, and Lydia will take over the day shift in the morning."

He made it sound like a production schedule for a factory. With time-and-a-half for overtime? Poor Simone would undoubtedly be expected to report for work as usual in the morning. Or was it considered that Simone might not need to stay on guard all night and could get some sleep herself once her charge had gone to sleep?

To sleep. To know no more. But they didn't know enough now, that was the trouble. How could this have happened? It wasn't the sort of decision a man took overnight. Oh, to walk out suddenly, perhaps. But that was for someone who had been subjected to intolerable pressure over a long period of time. Then, it might qualify as the "brainstorm" Simone kept diagnosing.

But, to walk away with all that money implied a long-term calculation, a deep dissatisfaction with his entire way of life, that must surely have cast some shadows ahead. And yet, he had never seemed discontented. Worried about the business at times, yes, but never about the quality of his home life. *Grace—that was becoming the part increasingly harder to face.*

"We'll work this out somehow." Harvey was still patting her hand abstractly. "We'll manage something."

"I'll be all right." She pulled her hand away. "I just need to be alone and—"

The doorbell blasted through their awkward silence in a sharp, peremptory burst, followed by another. While the others waited expectantly as Simone hurried forward to open the door, Karen leaned back and closed her eyes in relief. She knew who it was. Only one person ever rang the doorbell like that.

Her cousin, Jill Derwent, had come down, after all. And Jill would get rid of the others for her. With Jill staying the night, no one else would feel bound to. She was no longer being left all alone.

CHAPTER 8

I'M not sure," Jill said slowly, "that I believe one word of it."

Karen found such qualified reassurance like rain on parched soil compared to the torrent of trust and testimonials that had poured over her from the Board of Directors—while all their narrowed eyes watched for her reactions, waiting for some sign of betrayal. Jill *meant* what she said.

"It isn't *like* John. He could never even dream of doing such a thing—" Jill broke off and poured more coffee absently. It was obvious that she had suddenly come upon the blank wall which Karen had been facing for days.

Because it *had* happened. That was the implacable fact none of them could get around. No protests would change it. It was unthinkable—but the unthinkable was happening to people all the time, all over the world. Even at this moment, women were looking incredulously at policemen and crying out: *"Not my boy. Not my son. Not my husband.*

He's a good man. It isn't possible. It can't be true. There must be some mistake." In French, Spanish, in Japanese, in Norwegian, in German, in English, the ancient endless threnody went on.

"Let's take stock." Jill got down to practicalities. "How do *you* stand?"

"He's innocent," Karen said automatically. "There must be some mistake."

"No, dear," Jill said gently. "I don't mean that. I mean, how do you stand financially? You and John have a joint bank account, haven't you? How much is left in it? I mean—"

Has he cleaned that out, too? There was no delicate way of phrasing it.

"I don't know," Karen admitted. "It hadn't occurred to me to ask."

"Then that's the first thing we'd better find out." Jill made a note on the pad of paper beside her coffee cup, becoming brisker at the thought of something definite to be done. "You'd better ring up and find out—" She glanced at her watch. "As soon as the bank opens."

It was only 7:00 in the morning. Earlier, usually, than either of them would be up, but circumstances were unusual.

"The house is in my name alone," Karen said defensively. This compulsion to defend John, even from charges that had not yet been made, was new and rather frightening. But the whole situation was frightening.

"That's something," Jill said, making another note. "How does the mortgage stand?"

"I don't know." She had never realized before just how

much she did not know. "John always handled things like that."

"Then that's something else you'd better find out." Jill made another notation, carefully keeping her lashes lowered so that the expression in her eyes was hidden.

We can't all be practical. But that was unfair, because Jill was not only practical, she was the most talented textile designer Harding Handicrafts had ever let slip through their fingers. So good that she was still doing assignments for them after leaving to work on a freelance basis—which meant working for manufacturers, as well—a defection seldom forgiven. Perhaps being practical was a talent, too. Jill always had been practical, even as a child. So much so that her family was astounded when she eventually opted for art school along with Karen. They had expected her to become the perfect secretary—or possibly a chartered accountant.

"Any outstanding debts?" Jill met her eyes and sighed faintly. "That you know of," she added.

Karen shook her head apologetically and watched Jill put three question marks and an exclamation point on her notepad.

"I suppose I should have paid more attention to these things," Karen said. "But there never seemed to be any real reason why I should."

"No," Jill agreed. "There never is—until it's too late. If you didn't realize that, John should have. Especially with all the flying back and forth to the Continent he's been doing. Anything could have happened at any time. In any case, every wife ought to be up to date on the financial situation of the family. It's just plain *criminal* not to—" She broke off in confusion.

Criminal. That was the first time the word had actually been uttered.

"I'm sorry," Jill said quickly. "I didn't mean—"

"I know," Karen said. "Let's not worry about little things like that. At least, you're trying to help. I—I'll probably hear a lot worse than that . . . if John doesn't come home soon."

Jill gave her a swift look, then nodded and returned her attention to the notepad. "Outstanding credits?" she asked. "What about your salary—And John's? Salary is still paid a month in arrears, isn't it? Have your cheques—?"

"At least I know our salaries," Karen told her, grateful for a question she could answer. She watched Jill jot down the figures. "The last cheque transfers should have gone through. But I don't know—it's mid-month now. I don't know what they'll do about—"

"Neither do I," Jill admitted. "They ought to pay *your* salary, of course, but—"

Another awkward question. Did a firm pay the salary of a defaulting executive for the most recent time worked? During which time it must be presumed he was more actively engaged in the intricacies of working out the final details of his plans than in transacting company business? The world was full of awkward questions now.

"I've brought down some new designs," Jill said. "So I'll have to be going over there this morning. Perhaps I can find out." She tore off the sheet of paper and began a fresh page. "It will be less awkward if I do the asking."

A foot in both camps. But that was unfair, too. Jill was being marvellous, and she couldn't have had much sleep last night if she had been working out all these questions in her mind. And it was quite true. They were all questions that would have to be answered sooner or later. And, if Jill didn't ask them, then who?

"Have you notified your solicitor?"

"No." Karen pushed back her chair, no longer able to sit still. "No. It's too soon—No. It—" Automatically, she began heading for her studio.

"All right." Jill followed after her, carrying the notepad. "We don't have to worry about that right now. Perhaps it *is* too soon."

Karen found a lump of clay and began working with it. Independently of her conscious mind, her knuckles made indentations, her fingers smoothed and shaped, finding their own solace in the cool familiar clay.

"How about insurance policies?" Jill relentlessly pursued the spectre of financial solvency. "Do you both have them? What are the terms? They haven't been borrowed on, have you?"

"I don't know." Her fingers tore at the clay. "I don't think so. I mean—I don't think I could collect anything on them—" Insurance companies didn't insure wives against decamping husbands. Perhaps it was a sideline they ought to look into.

"Your jewellery? You inherited some quite nice Victorian pieces from your grandmother." Jill looked up, met her gaze and flushed, but persisted. "I suppose you know where they all are?"

"In the bank. In the safe deposit box." But John had been in the bank last week. The bearer bonds from the Company file were missing.

"You've checked recently?" Jill seemed to be aware of

this. She must have had quite a conversation when she went to the door with the Board of Directors last night. It hadn't seemed to take much time, but obviously it had covered all the salient points.

"No. I wore the garnets to the Staff Dinner Dance on New Year's Eve. I haven't seen them since." She hesitated. "John put them back in the safe deposit box for me."

Or did Grace like jewellery?

"I see." Jill was carefully noncommittal, but she made another note before she looked up. "You *do* have a key to the safe deposit box?"

"Yes, of course." She was grateful for another redeeming answer in the face of Jill's growing disapproval.

"Well, thank heavens for that," Jill murmured, not quite under her breath.

Jill was right, that was the trouble. It had been terribly lazy and careless of her not to have taken any notice of their financial position. But John should have known better, as well. He should have taken some time and forced her to pay attention.

Especially if—She pulled her mind away from that thought. Naturally, a man didn't say to his wife, *"I'm planning to abscond tomorrow, dear, so come and sit down while I go over the budget with you, so that you can know where you stand."*

No, a man didn't tell his wife a thing like that. *Not unless he were planning to take her with him.* Karen felt a sudden agonizing wrench of pain.

"The furniture is all paid for," she told Jill quickly. "Except for the television set, which is rented, and the deep freeze which has two more quarterly payments due."

"That's right," Jill encouraged. "That's much better. Now you're beginning to function again."

To what purpose? She smiled wanly at Jill, who was doing her best to help in the only way she could. It wasn't Jill's fault that this terrible thing had happened.

"Can you think of anything else?" Jill urged. "If you can't, don't worry. It will all come back to you gradually." She sounded as though she were encouraging the first steps of a convalescent after a long and debilitating illness.

"I'll try." Karen tried to sound co-operative because it really seemed to matter to Jill. "Perhaps things *will* come back."

But would John? That was the question. Her fingers pulled and prodded at the clay.

"Things can hardly get any worse," Jill said. "Or can they?" she added slowly.

Karen became aware that Jill was staring at the figure beneath her fingers with growing consternation. She looked down at it herself.

Curled beneath her fingers lay a small perfect representation of a human form. No bigger than a kitten, exact in every detail, eyes closed, faintly dreaming smile curving the tiny mouth, it curled up against itself tightly, yet relaxed, obviously patiently awaiting its moment to be born: a foetus.

"Oh Lord!" Jill said. "Don't tell me you're—"

"No." Karen stared down at it as though hypnotized. No, they had postponed the idea. Talked it over and decided to wait another year or two, until the business was fully on its feet again and they could devote enough time—

Time. Once there had been all the time in the world. Once there had been a future stretching out before them.

Before both of them. And now, so suddenly, time had run out and there was no more future left.

"No." Hardly knowing what she did, Karen raised her hand above the clay, clenched it and—

"Don't destroy it!" Jill's hand darted in and scooped the figure out of the way of Karen's descending fist.

"It's good. It's very good." Jill cradled the figure in her own hands, studying it. "You'll want to fire it some day— preserve it."

"I won't," Karen said.

"You might. You'll feel differently about it later. It *is* very good, you know."

"I won't," Karen said again.

"You don't mean—?" Jill looked up. "Then Grace—?" Shades of Derek's "brainstorms" passed like shadows between them.

"Was Grace pregnant? Was that why—?"

"I don't know," Karen said. For the first time, the tears came. "I don't know."

CHAPTER 9

S HE waited until Jill had left for the offices of Harding Handicrafts before starting out for the bank. Ordinarily she didn't miss the car when John was using it. They were only a ten-minute stroll from the High Street and she enjoyed the walk when the weather was good.

Now she found herself moving at a snail's pace, trying not to think. The car, the company car, would presumably be repossessed by the company—when it was found. And when it was found—if it were found—would John be found with it? Would they ever find the car? How could they, by themselves, without professional help? But if they reported it to the police and gave them the licence number, then the police could put out an alert for it. There was then a good chance of some patrol car spotting it—somewhere in the country—if John were still using it.

But Harding Handicrafts couldn't do that without giving the police a reason. And that was a step none of them was prepared to take. Not yet.

The bank loomed just ahead of her and she had to steady herself with a conscious effort before she walked into it. Inside, she hesitated, trying to nerve herself to the task of asking the question, controlling her voice. Perhaps she ought to try the safe deposit box first—

Her usual teller looked up, caught her eye, and smiled. Too late—she was trapped, the decision made for her. She smiled back unsteadily and crossed to the window. She could do it. She had done it dozens of times before—when the answer didn't really matter.

"Could you tell me—?" Concentrating on holding her voice steady, she lost the train of thought and had to start again.

"I'm afraid I've been writing cheques again without filling in the counterfoil." It was too apologetic, too nervous, but he didn't seem to notice. He was still smiling; she had done this before.

"I'm afraid I've hopelessly lost track. Could you let me know how much I—we—have in our account?"

"Certainly, Mrs. Randolph." As though it were the most natural thing in the world—which it had been . . . once—he turned and left the counter.

In a moment he was back, sliding a discreetly folded compliments slip across the counter to her. The amount would be jotted inside. He was still smiling. She forced herself not to unfold the paper, not to look until she could do so in privacy. The safe deposit box would ensure her that.

" . . . very warm," he was saying.

"Yes, very," she agreed. Was the account in credit then? His attitude hadn't changed—not that it would be likely to. The account had been very low at times before, but new salary cheques were always on the way. He wasn't to know that that wouldn't be the case this time. He'd assume everything was all right, even if the account was showing an overdraft. She must not try to read anything into his attitude.

And he couldn't read anything into hers. She felt obscurely comforted by that, realizing for the first time that outsiders were not aware of what had happened. Not yet. It was her own personal cataclysm. So long as she kept moving, smiling, speaking, with some semblance of normalcy, they could not guess. They could not tell just by looking at her.

She moved slowly across the smooth marble floor of the bank to the grille gate that locked off the vault. The guard smiled at her and opened the gate.

A for abandoned. D for deserted. The initials were not branded across her forehead, nor marked on her features. The scars were deep inside her at the moment. How much time did she have before the Board of Directors would decide that their uneasy secret could no longer be kept and her wounds would be exposed to public view?

The barred gate swung back and she walked into the vault. The official there matched her key with his own and removed the safe deposit box. He carried it to an empty cubicle, placed it on the table, smiled at her and left, gently closing the door behind him. She sank into the chair and stared at the box for a moment.

Pandora's box. What new evils would she let loose upon the world—upon herself—when she opened it? She shrank from the thought. But she could not go home and face Jill and admit that she had lacked the courage even to look inside the box. Not when she had forced herself to come this far.

She was still holding the folded slip of paper. She dropped it beside the box where it looked equally menacing, both posing a further threat to her peace of mind. What was left of it. In fact, so little remained that one or two more blows would scarcely signify. Jill was right—it was better to know the worst.

She stretched out her hand and flipped back the lid of the box. The small leather jewel cases lay on top of some papers. The case containing the garnets was nearest to her. She drew it out, took a deep breath, and opened it quickly before her courage could falter again.

A row of shining dark red stones blinked up at her before her eyes blurred with tears and she could no longer see them. She pushed the case aside quickly, still open, and reached for the next case unsteadily. Opals glittered with a life of their own from the eternal fire in their depths. She reached for the next case purely because Jill would expect her to; would be angry—no, exasperated—if she didn't check every case, even though there was no real need to now. She knew. They were all there. Nothing had been taken.

It was a formality, too, to unfold the slip of paper and check the amount written inside. Plenty. Contrary to her statement to the teller, she had not been writing any cheques lately. Neither, it appeared, had John. The account was well in the black. He could not even have taken any of his travel allowance with him.

Why should he—for a weekend trip that was to be mainly a series of business conferences?

A faint stirring of warmth began to flicker, the beginning of a returning strength.

Not abandoned—entirely. *Not* deserted—with any real finality. So, back to square one, with more conviction now. There must be some mistake. There must be some reasonable explanation.

Yes, even for Grace.

However, John had visited this bank, been shown into a cubicle similar to this, taking with him the assets being held for Harding Handicrafts, and now a quarter of a million pounds in bearer bonds were missing—and so was John. It was rather hard to think of a reasonable explanation for that.

Thoughtfully she returned her attention to the deposit box, drawing out the papers and documents at the bottom and sorting through them meticulously. Their marriage certificate, the deeds to the house, their wills—each leaving everything to the other—a few share certificates, all in order.

It had been a silly idea. Everything was the same. Nothing had been taken away, nothing had been added. But it had been well to check. If the question were ever to come up, she could deal with it now.

Slowly she gathered the papers together and replaced them in the box. Carefully she placed the jewel cases on top in the order in which they had been removed and closed the lid. She refolded the slip of paper and tucked it into her handbag.

Unfinished business. The thought slid into her mind as though it had been left down here in the vault to wait for her. Ridiculous to imagine it some sort of telepathic message from John, and yet she could not completely fight the impulse to do so.

Fight. Was that another message? Or simply her common sense reasserting itself at last? But who did you fight? And how?

Not the people at Harding Handicrafts. They couldn't be blamed for thinking the worst. And, despite their suspicions—or because of them—they were doing their best to help.

Perhaps the best thing might be to start with the suddenly unknown quantity. *Grace.*

27 Swansdowne Crescent, Flat 2. The address had obviously been hovering at the edge of her consciousness for some time now. It sprang sharply to the fore. Even the telephone number began emerging—and she had not thought she knew it well enough to remember it. She had only dialled it a few times to deliver messages from John about office matters.

There would be no point in telephoning—the number began to recede—there would be no one there to take a call. However, it could do no harm to walk over to Swansdowne Crescent and just look around . . .

Absently, she admired the deft efficiency with which her mind slid away from the thought that she knew where the spare key was to be found which would let her into the flat. Once before, she had had to go over there to collect some papers. The hiding place wouldn't have changed. People don't change their hiding places, they leave keys there so that their friends will know where to find them.

Karen stood, picked up the safe deposit box and let herself out of the cubicle, closing the door quietly behind her.

The guard looked up, a trace of relief on his face revealing that he must have begun to worry. How long had she been in there? She could not look at her watch right now, that would be a dead giveaway that she had lost track of time. She could only smile and hand over the box smoothly, as though she were unaware of his anxiety.

The guard returned her smile, reassured, and locked her box into its place in the vault. "Hot day today." He gave back her key. "I often think it would be a good idea if people with boxes came in here where it's cool and took a breather on a day like this. They'd feel better for it."

"I know I do." She gave him the answer he wanted, knowing that her appearance must have improved. He had found an explanation he could accept—she had been looking pale and unwell when she came in because the heat had been affecting her. A visit—rest, really, since she had remained longer than usual—to the cool vault had revived her. It certainly had, but not in any way he could understand.

A final exchange of smiles and she turned away, moving with a sense of purpose, to the next destination she had in mind. *Grace.*

CHAPTER 10

THE key hung from a string on the inside of the letter-slot in the front door. Quite conventional—just like Grace. And that was a thought. Surely Grace was too conventional to run away with another woman's husband? Or was the secretary-and-employer situation so conventional that it seemed almost respectable? In its way, it was as classic as the key-on-a-latchstring behind the mail slot.

The door swung open and Karen stepped inside. She lost the sensation of being an intruder as she advanced into the living-room. The empty flat was neither hostile nor friendly. It was simply there—as she was there—both of them with a job to do, jobs that were now hanging in a curious state of suspension while the people who were the reasons for them were absent.

She looked around helplessly. What had she possibly thought an empty flat could tell her? And yet . . . little random oddities tugged at her attention: a tumbled pile of long-playing records, their empty sleeves beside them in an equally tumbled pile, by the record-player; the cushions vaguely askew on the sofa; some of the desk drawers not quite closed. An uneasy feeling impelled her into the bedroom behind the living-room.

Again, there was nothing immediately discernible. Certainly nothing that told its occupant had left not expecting to return. A pair of comfortable bedroom slippers lay just inside the door, waiting to be stepped into as shoes were kicked off at the end of a weary day. A book lay on the bedside table, its bookmark showing that it was only half read.

Karen crossed the room slowly, drawn by the closet and bureau on the other side. Not that she had enough idea of the extent of Grace's wardrobe to be able to determine how many garments she had packed, but surely she ought to be able to tell *something*—

She swung open the closet door. A solidly-packed row of hanging clothes faced her. It took a moment to discern that there were about three empty coat-hangers on the rack. A row of footwear was ranged neatly below the clothing, small gaps denoting that possibly two pairs of shoes were missing.

A message *was* beginning to emerge from the silent flat. It grew louder in the kitchen where an upturned cup, saucer and plate on the draining board gave evidence of a breakfast eaten and the dishes hastily rinsed and left to dry by themselves.

The fridge, too, told its own story. Butter, eggs, cottage cheese, salad vegetables beginning to wilt, a pint of milk which had reached the curdled stage of looking very sorry for itself. A few other items which could reasonably have been expected to survive a weekend, but which would not have been left indefinitely. Not by someone so tidy and responsible as Grace.

Karen shut the door and turned away from the fridge. Perhaps the evidence she had found was too inconclusive to convince anyone else—perhaps she was building too much on an admittedly insufficient knowledge of her subject, but she didn't think so.

Grace had intended to return to this flat. Like John, she had planned on no more than a weekend's absence—a business weekend. Whatever had happened had not been premeditated and cold-bloodedly planned out. At least, not by Grace.

A brainstorm? Simone's theory seemed the only possible one in these circumstances, and yet she could not credit it. Such a brainstorm would have had to strike two thoroughly responsible, completely adult people at the same moment and with enough force to convince that all was well thrown away for the sudden impulse.

It wasn't possible—not with John and Grace. Or rather, the manner of it was not possible. If such a temptation had arisen, neither of them would have counted the world well lost for it. They would have returned quietly from the momentous weekend, settled back into their accustomed routines, and made plans to find a way to get the best of both worlds.

Of course, some people might call walking away with a quarter of a million pounds in bearer bonds a well-made plan to get the best of both worlds.

Karen moved restlessly. Walking back to the bedroom

again, she stared down at the waiting bedroom slippers. Comfortable, slightly heeled-over, beginning to lose their shape, they did not resemble anything that would be worn by a secret *femme fatale*. They looked, in fact, rather like Grace herself, plain and dependable. To be trusted—not suspected. John had trusted Grace and liked her—those were his only emotions concerning her.

Aimlessly, Karen's gaze drifted from the slippers across the room to the bureau. She had not explored that. Should she? Something about the drawers was already invitingly vulnerable—not quite ajar, but certainly not closed so tightly as they ought to have been—and drew her. Wasn't that unlike Grace? Wouldn't Grace have shut every drawer firmly and neatly?

And yet . . . the desk drawers in the living-room had also been faintly awry. Unable to resist the magnet, she allowed herself to be pulled across the room.

Like the drawer itself, the contents of the first drawer were just faintly awry in a disorder that would not have signified anything to anyone who was not aware of Grace's excessive tidiness. Karen checked the other drawers with the sinking feeling which had grown so familiar during the past few days.

All the drawers had been disturbed. Not blatantly—rather as though a careful burglar had gone through them searching for items of value, but loath to leave any obvious traces of his pillage.

Two sweaters jumbled together on top of the plastic bags that would normally have encased them were the extent of his carelessness.

A professional. Probably one who operated "on spec,"

who had found the latchkey in its classic hiding place an open invitation to come in and take a look around.

Karen closed the drawers and wandered back into the living-room, realizing her helplessness. She could not call the police—she would be unable to tell them what, if anything, was missing. To do so would also be to admit that she had gained illegal entry to the flat, and any explanation would set them to investigating more than the burglary.

There was, in fact, nothing at all that she could do. With a sense of futility—of, perhaps, missing something important because she had no idea what she ought to be looking for—she glanced around the room for the last time. Then, listening quietly at the door for a moment to make sure no one was in the hallway outside, she opened the door, stepped out quickly and shut it behind her.

All the way home she was haunted by the feeling that there was something more she ought to have done, ought to have noticed. The feeling almost obliterated the earlier relief she had experienced in the bank vault. For every question that seemed settled, another seemed to open up in its place.

CHAPTER 11

KAREN was in the studio working when she heard the front door slam. That would be Jill coming back. Jill was always in too much of a hurry to close a door properly, it always seemed to slip from her fingers as she rushed along to more important matters.

"Karen? Are you home?"

"Is she here?" Before Karen could answer, the other voice cut in.

"I don't know." Jill's voice held a trace of impatience, as though she were holding herself back from pointing out that, as they had just come together, she could hardly be expected to possess any more information than her companion. "Karen?" she called again.

Karen threw a cloth over the clay she had been working and moved slowly towards the studio door. She wished Jill had returned alone, she was not in the mood for company right now.

"Jill—" The timbre of Harvey's voice suddenly

changed. About to open the door and join them, Karen hesitated.

"Jill, I'd like to take this opportunity to say that I'm very glad that you're here to help Karen through this trying time."

"Yes. Perhaps I ought to see if she's upstairs. She may be asleep—"

"I think it's wonderful of you to come down here and stand by her in her hour of need." As they all knew to their cost, once Harvey was in a valedictory mood it was almost impossible to shut him off.

"She *is* my cousin," Jill said crisply.

"That's what I mean. Of course, we're all trying to do our best for her, but there's nothing like having your blood-kin around you at a time like this."

"I really *had* better check upstairs." Sometimes evasive action worked. Karen could sense Jill's growing desperation.

"No, don't rush off. You English are always rushing off—" A more sensitive man than Harvey might have begun to identify cause and effect. Karen put her hand on the doorknob, about to turn it and go to Jill's rescue.

"I want to talk to you seriously." His tone was the one which was invariably accompanied by a vice-like grip on the victim's forearm. "About Karen."

Karen's hand fell away from the doorknob.

"What about Karen?" Jill asked.

"She's taking this awfully well, isn't she?" Harvey lowered his voice meaningly. "She doesn't seem too upset at all."

"Karen isn't the sort to have hysterics." Jill's voice was

cold. "I think we can safely assume she's upset, however."

"Yes, but *how* upset?"

"Now, see here—" Jill's voice rose angrily. "If you're trying to insinuate that she had anything to *do* with—"

"No, no, nothing of the sort." Harvey backtracked hastily. "I only meant . . . well, she's *too* quiet. Still waters run deep—and you never could tell what she was thinking. And now she's quieter than ever . . . in the face of all this . . ." His voice trailed off unhappily.

"Oh, really!" Jill said. It was as much as she could say without admitting that Karen was only *that* quiet with people she didn't particularly like.

"Yes, yes, I know." He was placating now. "Part of it is her artistic temperament. You have a good bit of it yourself—"

"Harvey, I really don't think—"

"That's why I'm so glad you're here. You can understand her, keep an eye on her—"

"An eye—?"

"That's what worries me," Harvey confessed. "I thought of it last night—just as I was going to sleep—and I haven't had a wink of sleep since."

"Harvey—"

"*You* don't think—" his voice dropped lower—"*you* don't think she'd *do* anything, do you?"

"*Do* anything?" But Jill's tone was just faintly wrong. Harvey seized on the uncertain note with relief.

"Then it isn't just my imagination. You've thought of it, too."

"Harvey, I don't know what you're talking about, or what you've been thinking about." Jill's voice grew firmer. "But I can assure you—"

Karen opened the door. If she hadn't known they had merely been discussing her, she could have suspected them of a lot worse.

"Karen!" Jill moved away from Harvey so rapidly that he had no time to relinquish his grip on her forearm. His arm moved with her, giving the impression that he was thrusting her away.

"I thought I heard voices," Karen smiled at them innocently. "I'm afraid I've been asleep."

"Good idea!" Harvey said. "You need to rest all you can at a time like this—" Catching a poisonous glance from Jill he broke off. "I mean—"

"I thought you might be," Jill said smoothly, a flicker of her eyelids betraying that she didn't for one moment believe it, but would observe the polite conventions. "I was just telling Harvey so."

"Hello, Harvey," Karen said.

"I guess you must think I'm like the bad penny, always turning up, hey?" Harvey said.

The remark was too unfortunately apt to risk commenting on. Karen gave a noncommittal smile.

"I'll tell you," Harvey went on. "I was just leaving the office and I met Jill—just leaving, too. And I thought, why don't I go and take those two gals out to dinner? I'm at a loose end right now, you know." He smiled wistfully. "A grass widower. Olive has taken the boys back to get them outfitted for school. It starts after the first weekend in September, and she thought she ought to be there with them for the first few weeks. Oh, she's right, of course. It's left me a bit high and dry—but I do see her point. Olive," he added unnecessarily, "is in the States right now."

Olive usually was. Curiously, the company did not seem to feel that this made her less admirable as a company wife. Quite the contrary, it seemed to feel that an American-oriented wife was the ideal—she kept her husband's eye firmly on his home base, his mind fixed on his "roots" and, perhaps most important, it dispelled any temptation he might have to settle down in a comfortable foreign billet and "go native."

"So, I'm at your service, ladies—" He spread his hands. "Anywhere you'd like to go. We can sample the delicacies at one of the local bistros, or we can go farther afield—even up to London, if you like. Just tell me your wish—I'm yours to command."

"I'm not hungry," Karen said flatly.

"Oh, but you *must* eat." His consternation was as great as though she had suddenly announced she were embarking on a hunger strike. "You've got to keep going."

"Perhaps," Jill intervened delicately, "we can think it over. You've sprung this on us rather suddenly, after all, Harvey—"

So Jill had not had any idea that this was what Harvey had had in mind when he joined her.

"Why don't we sit down," Jill suggested. "We can have a drink and discuss it."

"Fine, fine," Harvey said. He looked at his watch. "But we ought to get going fairly soon, you know. Places will be booked out if we wait too long."

"You can phone from here." Heedless of his anxiety, Jill began pouring drinks.

"Yes, fine." Harvey appeared mesmerized by his watch. "But I think—" He slid a sideways glance at Karen and returned his attention to his watch. "I mean, we don't want to be late."

"How can we be late when we haven't booked anywhere?" Jill asked reasonably.

"That's right," Harvey said. "You're absolutely right." He darted another glance at Karen.

"Here—" Jill handed him his drink. "For heaven's sake, sit down and relax."

"Yes, thanks." He took it and perched on the edge of an armchair. His gaze jittered from his watch to Karen and back again.

"Harvey," Karen said. "I'm beginning to have the feeling that there's something you want to tell me." It could not be anything good, she knew, or he would have blurted it out the instant he saw her. She braced herself for a fresh blow.

"Well, that is—" Harvey said. "Speaking of restaurants, it reminded me—" He broke off as their blank looks told him that they had not actually been speaking of restaurants.

"No, that isn't strictly accurate," he corrected himself. "To tell you the truth, Simone reminded me this morning. I wouldn't have thought of it—" He loosened his tie.

They both continued staring at him, refusing to help him.

"Well, it's John's cards," he said awkwardly. "His credit cards. Do you know where they are, Karen?"

"Credit cards?" The thought of them had never crossed her mind. They seemed the least of her problems.

"*You* know—American Express, Diners Club, Barclaycard, Airlines—he had them all. I—we—Simone— Well, if he had left them here with you, fair enough. You can keep them and go on using them. We certainly wouldn't dream of—"

"I don't know where they are," Karen said. "I imagine

he was carrying them with him. He usually did. That was the point of having them, wasn't it?"

"Oh yes, yes," Harvey said. "I quite agree. Ordinarily—" He found himself floundering in deep water again.

"I see," Karen said slowly.

"Of course you do." Harvey sounded relieved. "Circumstances being what they are, we'll have to do something. All those cards mean he has considerable credit at his disposal— and the company footing the bill. Why, that Airlines Card alone means he could board a flight to Rio de Janeiro and—" Harvey's voice choked with outrage—"*we'd* have to pay for it! We wouldn't even know about it until the bills came in. And by then it would be too late to trace—"

She hadn't said a word. She had even stopped looking at him.

"I'm sorry, Karen. I didn't mean— Oh my God!" He worried his tie once more and looked at Jill pleadingly.

"It's all right, Harvey." Jill spoke with the determined cheerfulness of a professional nurse trying to buoy up a sinking patient. "Karen understands. But something like this takes a great deal of facing up to."

"It sure does!" Harvey agreed heartily. "It hasn't been easy for any of us, either. To realize that someone we've respected and trusted—"

"Harvey," Jill cut in. "Let me get you another drink."

"But I haven't finished this one—Oh!" He sank into a depressed silence, meekly relinquishing his glass.

"There." Jill topped it up briskly and handed it back. Tactfully she ignored the fact that Karen hadn't touched hers.

"But you've got to see—" Harvey came back to the fray,

moving his foot a fraction of an instant before Jill brought her heel down where it had been.

"Believe me, Karen, we want to do all we can to help, but we've got to cover ourselves as well. I feel we can handle this without too much difficulty by just cancelling those credit cards. That's why I wanted to make certain that you didn't have them before I authorized such a step. It's perfectly simple and we can manage it without mentioning John at all. We can just say the cards have been stolen. It happens all the time. They have a whole procedure geared to just that contingency."

Stolen. Karen winced visibly.

"It's routine, automatic." Harvey went on trying to offer comfort. "There's no need for anyone to know any more than that. They won't think twice about—"

"Harvey," Jill said. "Am I mistaken, or did I think I heard you offer us dinner a while ago?"

"Right, that's right!" Harvey glared at his watch, all his former preoccupation with time and food reasserting itself under this gentle probing. "And I don't know about you two, but I'm getting pretty damned hungry. Why don't we drive out to the—"

"You and Jill go," Karen said. "I'm not hungry."

"Oh, now, we can't have that," Harvey protested. "We can't go off and leave you here all alone—brooding."

"I won't brood," Karen said. "At least, not the way you mean." She wanted more time to think. She regretted that she could not send Harvey packing so that she could have a private consultation with Jill. She could not discuss her afternoon in front of Harvey. He would be upset—probably shocked —by her visit to Grace's flat. Worse, he would consider her discoveries too nebulous—and too negative—to be of any value. Nor was it likely that he would believe in any burglary. He would consider it imagination—or possibly even a crude attempt on her part to try to divert suspicion from John.

"Look at the time!" Harvey seemed genuinely upset. "If we don't get started now, we'll never get in anywhere. We'd better—" he stood up—"be on our way."

Karen didn't move. Jill put down her drink and gathered up the jacket she had tossed over a chair when she came in. Either she was in the mood to go out, or she felt Harvey would be less of a tactless menace if he were able to put some food into his mouth every time he opened it—rather than his foot.

"Come on, Karen." Harvey frowned at his watch again. "You'll feel better after you've eaten."

"Yes, Karen." Jill's glance threatened dire revenge if she were left to go out alone with Harvey. "You must." Her tone left Karen no option.

"That's right." Harvey stretched out a hand and helped Karen unnecessarily to her feet. "I've got the car right outside and we can—"

One moment there had been no one in sight—suddenly Simone and Derek were coming through the french windows.

"Ah, Kaa-ren, we are finding you home." Simone gave a small insincere smile. "That is good."

"We—We were just leaving." Harvey seemed taken aback. "Right this minute. We were going out to dinner."

"We will not keep you. It is nothing of great importance." With an imperious gesture, Simone swept Derek forward. He was carrying a covered bowl. "I am making an egg custard for you. I think you will like it."

"That's very kind of you," Karen said faintly. "But, really, you shouldn't have bothered."

"Oh, it wasn't any bother," Derek rushed to assure her. "Simone made one for us, too. She's been using up some extra milk. I wish it happened more often—she's a jolly good cook, and her egg custards are delicious."

"Derek, perhaps you will place it in the refrigerator for Karen." Simone did not appear to appreciate his tribute to her culinary prowess. "You will do it now."

"Oh, certainly. Of course." Bewildered, Derek backed towards the kitchen, aware that he had somehow transgressed, but unsure how. Or, perhaps more accurately—how Simone had discovered his latest transgression—whoever she was.

"You are looking well, Karen." Simone turned a scarcely less steely gaze on her and then on Harvey. "You have told her yet?"

"I asked her," Harvey admitted. "She hasn't seen them. He must have all his credit cards with him."

"Then we will cancel them in the morning." Simone nodded decisively. "We should have done so days ago. This is as I have suspected."

"I wonder if she's counted the petty cash yet," Jill murmured under her breath.

Karen smiled faintly, realizing again how much Jill's presence was heartening her. How did people without relatives manage?

"I've put it in the fridge." Derek came back into the room, smiling ingratiatingly at Karen. "I'm sure you'll like it." He avoided his wife's unforgiving gaze.

"I'm sure I will." What else could she say? It was hardly

the moment to confess that she loathed egg custard—it had been John who had liked it. She retreated from that thought. Simone could not have known that—she was trying to be kind. It was a pity she was so irritating.

There was an awkward silence.

"I'll tell you what—" Harvey broke in desperately. "Why don't you folks join us for dinner? It won't be any trouble—we haven't made reservations. Come along and we'll take pot luck somewhere."

"I do not think—" Simone began severely.

"If you're sure it won't be any trouble—" Derek said eagerly. It was obvious that he was not looking forward to going home with Simone and discovering what new sins had found him out.

"Yes, do," Jill seconded. "It will make it more of a party." And, incidentally, relieve the strain of trying to keep up a conversation with Harvey, who was heavy weather at the best of times.

"Yes, come," Karen said, a sudden compassion for Derek overcoming her distaste for Simone. He would have a hard enough time when he *did* have to go home.

"Say, this is a great idea." Harvey was elated with the success of his suggestion. "What a good thing you people happened to come along. The more the merrier—"

Simone stopped him dead with a glance.

"Well, as much as possible, I mean. Things being—" He glanced apologetically at Karen and abdicated. "I'll go start the car," he said. "You people come along when you're ready."

CHAPTER 12

WHEN Karen awoke in the morning, Jill had already gone. A note on the kitchen table said that she would be at Harding Handicrafts all day, but expected to be back for dinner. Jill had not needed to add that there was no news. If there had been, she would have awakened Karen and told her.

No news *isn't* good news.

Absently, Karen heated up the coffee Jill had left and made toast. There had been no chance to talk to Jill last night—and now she would be out of reach all day. Not that there was much Jill could do, other than provide a sympathetic ear. The police were the only ones who could do anything now, and Karen was trying to steel herself to the disapproval of the Company if she called them in.

Last night she had mentally debated telling everyone then and there of her discoveries and trying to persuade them to her own convictions. But Harvey's ponderous jollities and Simone's glacial civility had defeated her. Derek had been pouring compliments over a semi-flirtatious Jill and Simone had grown more glacial still. It had been no time for special pleading, even if she had been wholly convinced that such a course was wise.

And yet, she was either going to have to go to the police herself, or else face the Board of Directors, present her evidence to them—and insist that the police be brought into the case. There was not much more that she could do alone.

She had just finished breakfast when the telephone rang. Even before she picked up the receiver she had the dismal feeling that she knew who was going to be on the other end of the line and she was right.

"Karen, honey, *there* you are!" Lydia said. "I tried all day yesterday to get you and I couldn't."

"I was out," Karen said unhelpfully. Poor Lydia—she must have had some agonizing moments wondering if the bird had flown.

"Well, look, honey, I'm going shopping," Lydia declared. "I think you ought to come along. Let's you and me make a day of it. We can start out now, have lunch at—"

Everyone was trying to feed her. Did she look that hungry?

"Thank you, Lydia," she said firmly, "but I have work to do."

"I know, and I think it's just marvellous the way you're taking this. 'Carrying on regardless'—it's *so* English."

"I *am* English." But Lydia would not be halted.

"Now Harvey told me y'all were out to dinner with him last night and I was just delighted to hear it. I *do* think it's sensible of you to behave like that."

"Lydia—"

"That's why I think it would be good for you to get away for the day and relax and enjoy yourself and just forget about everything—"

As though a missing husband were on a level with a toothache or something spilled on a favourite dress, ruining it.

"Lydia, I'm afraid I can't possibly do that."

"Honey, you fret too much. You're too conscientious, I've always said so. It won't make a particle of difference if you don't do any work on that tea-party set today and you know it. The work will still be there in the morning and you can go to it all the more refreshed for having taken a day off."

Lydia's tone had altered slightly. It was the Chairman's wife speaking now and her suggestion was tantamount to an order.

"I'm sorry, Lydia, I really have other things to do."

"*Do?*" Lydia spoke smoothly over the protest. "Honey, what on earth do you *have* to do? I just told you there's no hurry on that tea service. You can take all the time in the world over it—we can always put off the department store. They never expect orders from England on time anyway."

"I mean, I have some personal business to attend to." Too late, Karen realized that, in the present circumstance, that could be interpreted as meaning that she was packing her bags for an imminent flight to join John in some distant country which didn't have an Extradition Treaty with Britain. Lydia's immediate reaction reminded her.

"Now look, honey, you don't want to make any decisions too quickly, you know. It's the worst possible thing at a time like this. Why don't I come over and we can discuss—"

"Not today." There was nothing she wanted less than any sort of discussion with Lydia.

"Well then, you come over to dinner tonight—you and Jill." Lydia would not give up. "Now, I won't take 'no' for an answer." The steely note was back in her voice. "After all, you let Harvey take you out last night. If you don't let Vernon and me entertain you tonight, we'll be mortally offended. Now, promise you'll come."

"All right." The line of least resistance was the easiest way to get rid of Lydia. At least she would have Jill along for moral support later in the day. And she was going to have to talk seriously with Vernon Vandergreit in any case in one last attempt to gain his approval before contacting the police.

"That's fine. We'll expect you about seven, y'hear?"

"I hear." But the acknowledgment was unnecessary. Having gained her point, Lydia had immediately rung off.

Thoughtfully, Karen replaced the receiver. What could be the reason for this mad passion on everyone's part to feed her? Was it some version of funeral meats—?

She pulled her mind abruptly away from that trail of thought. Better to think simply that the people at Harding Handicrafts were exceptionally kind and thoughtful. Far more so, perhaps, than one might ordinarily expect them to be. Would she have been so hospitable and forbearing to one whose husband had presumably decamped with such a large sum? She doubted it. Not without a strong ulterior motive.

Of course, there was still the possibility that John might contact her, invite her to join him—wherever he was. (To set up a *ménage à trois* with Grace?) It might be unlikely, but it was obvious that the Vandergreits had not ruled out the possibility entirely, therefore their constant tender concern for her comfort—and whereabouts. And a meal was the best excuse for keeping her under surveillance for an evening.

She could not blame them. Were their positions reversed, she might be exercising the same careful concern over Lydia's movements. Hers might have been the solicitous voice on the telephone, the anxious presence hovering nearby, keeping tactful watch on Lydia's plans and reactions.

Karen found this a momentarily soothing thought—it was a pity the positions *weren't* reversed.

With a faint sigh, she turned away from the telephone intending to go into the studio and begin work, but a shadow on the lawn caught her eye and she moved towards the french windows instead.

The shadow stood its ground, faintly sinister, as though waiting—or watching the house. Elongated, stretching across the lawn just in front of the windows, silently betraying that someone was standing at the corner of the house—had been standing there for some time. How long?

Silently Karen opened the french windows and stepped out on to the lawn.

He had turned and was looking in the opposite direction as she approached. Even from the back, she could see that her first instinctive hope was wrong. Not John. Shorter, stockier, even the set of his shoulders was wrong. A stranger.

Or, at least, someone she did not know well.

Her foot struck a pebble, sending it skittering against the outside wall of the house. The sound was slight, but he whirled in instantaneous reflex, facing her as though she were an enemy.

Startled, she recoiled. Momentarily, so did he. They gazed at each other with wary recognition, stretching their lips in meaningless smiles.

"Mrs. Randolph." He started to proffer his hand, then pulled it back and turned the gesture into a vaguely-sketched wave instead.

"Dr. Feltham." She waved back, as though they were greeting each other across a wide deep chasm. "How are you?"

And what are you doing here? Did Lydia send you?

"Uh, fine. Fine, thank you." He hesitated, as though hearing the unspoken questions and debating whether or not to answer them. "And you?"

"As well as can be expected." With a faint rueful grimace she threw the medical cliché at him. Let him make of it what he would—provided that Lydia and Vernon hadn't primed him with all the necessary back-ground information.

"Yes." He glanced at her sharply, his dark eyes suspicious and alert. "Perhaps we might go inside?"

The better to take my pulse?

"Of course," she said demurely. "Would you like a cup of coffee?"

"That would be fine." Again the suspicious glance. "Just fine." He followed her into the house. She left the french windows ajar and seated herself in the wing chair, making no move towards the kitchen.

Nor did he appear to expect her to. He paced restlessly before her chair for a few moments, then turned and announced, "I don't believe it!"

"Thank you," she said.

"I didn't mean it that way—" He brushed aside her gratitude. "I mean, I don't believe it of Grace."

She leaned forward to speak, but he cut her off again.

"I'm sorry. I didn't mean that the way it sounded, either. The fact is, Grace and I are engaged."

"Engaged!" A constricting band loosened around her heart.

"We were keeping it secret. Grace wanted to keep her job and thought her position would be stronger if no one got the idea that she might be leaving to start a family within the next few years. It seems the American directors have very old-fashioned views about such things, and she felt an unmarried woman would be given preference if there were a chance for promotion."

"Yes," Karen said. "The Vandergreits *do* think that way. Grace was right."

"But the Vandergreits would eventually have to return to the States," he said. "Or go on to reorganize some other subsidiaries. With them out of the way, the problem would disappear and we could get married without anyone worrying about the fact. She was sure that your husband would be left in charge of Harding Handicrafts and she knew he wouldn't mind a bit."

"Of course, he wouldn't," Karen said thankfully. Every word was reinforcing her belief in John, her certainty that somewhere there was an explanation beyond the shoddy obvious one that everyone else was so intent upon accepting. "He's always been in favour of maternity leaves without loss of tenure."

"Precisely! You see what I mean then—?" His gesture

was both compelling and assertive. "The rest of it—all this—*can't* be true. Grace wouldn't do such a thing to me."

"Nor would John to me."

They gazed at each other solemnly, a sense of partisanship flowing between them. The true believers—or the self-deceived?

"Then—" For the first time, his certainty seemed to waver. "Where *are* they?"

"I don't know."

"They might not even be together." He said it as though the thought ought to cheer them both.

"There's quite a lot missing . . ." A new thought came to her. John would never have stolen the bearer bonds. But Grace—?

It was often the quiet perfect secretary, respectable, a pillar of society, fond of animals, good to her family, who wound up shame-faced in the Sunday papers about to be marched away to serve a jail sentence for embezzlement. It might be worth trying to find out whether Grace had been giving away unusual sums of money or expensive presents.

"So I understand." He looked at her sardonically, catching her thought. "And your husband had better access than Grace to it."

For an instant, mutual suspicion and recrimination hung in the air, then he shrugged. "There's no point in second-guessing at this stage. First we have to find out what's actually happened."

"How do we do that?" She knew that his "we" indicated that he had no more intention of involving the police than had the Directors of Harding Handicrafts. She found that, from him, she did not mind this quite so much. He was involved as much as she was—*and* on the same side. They were both prepared to assume innocence rather than guilt.

At least, she was prepared to assume that John was innocent, while he was prepared to assume that Grace was. The two assumptions were not necessarily mutually compatible. Nevertheless, it was a large advance on standing alone.

"Grace," she offered tentatively, "didn't seem to have gone away prepared for any longer stay than a weekend. And neither did John." She caught his eye and flushed. "I—I checked her flat yesterday. There were no signs that she wasn't planning to return to it."

"You'd notice those sort of signs more than a man would, I suppose." He nodded and glanced at his watch. "Look, we'll need to decide a course of action—but it will have to be later. I must finish making my rounds. I'm late now."

For an instant, something stirred uneasily at the back of her mind.

"After my surgery tonight," he said firmly. "I can get here about nine o'clock."

"I'm going out to dinner. If you want to talk to me tonight, I'll try to be back by eleven. Otherwise, perhaps we'd best wait until morning."

"Eleven o'clock then." He brushed aside the alternative. "I'll be waiting for you here." He sketched another wave and stepped through the french windows, leaving her staring after him uneasily.

CHAPTER 13

"**H**ONESTLY, Karen," Lydia said, pouring coffee in the lounge, "I think you ought to consider it. You could do a lot worse."

You already have, her tone implied.

"Lydia is right." Reclining in an enormous chair which shifted with his every movement, Vernon nodded agreement. "Of course, we realize it's maybe a little soon for you to make that kind of decision right now, but it's not too soon for you to hold the idea in the back of your mind and let it germinate for a while. Life must go on, you know."

"That's what I always say," Lydia chimed in promptly. "Karen, you're still a young woman and you can't let this blight your life. If you'll just—"

Karen stopped listening again. Lydia and Vernon had been harping on the same theme all evening, their constant refrain being the idea of America as the perfect place to rebuild a shattered life. To start all over again—still under the auspices of Vandergreit Enterprises, of course—and rise to the heights of a dazzling career.

John had not been mentioned at all—except obliquely— during the evening. They had shut her off—smoothly but finally—every time she had tried to talk about him.

Jill was staring absently at a print of astounding awfulness hanging on the wall just above Vernon's head, probably contemplating the fitting justice of seeing it fall on that head, thus destroying the print and, with any luck, damaging Vernon as well. After several tries, Karen managed to catch her eye and moved her gaze pointedly to her wristwatch.

"We've had a lovely evening." Jill rose to her feet in a fluid motion, as though the signal had released her from a spell. "It's been most kind of you to have had us—"

"You're *not* going now?" Lydia gave a wail of anguish. "So soon? It seems as though you just got here."

Not to us. Karen avoided Jill's eyes, conscious of the thought flashing through their minds.

There had been no chance to talk to Jill before dinner. Jill had been kept busy at the office until the last moment and had been given a lift to the Vandergreits' by Vernon himself, undoubtedly acting on instructions from Lydia. Jill had no idea that Ian Feltham would be waiting for them back at the house.

In fact, if they could be back before he arrived, there would be time to explain new developments to Jill then.

"But I feel awful—" Lydia was still making hospitable noises. "You going off like this—I feel we've offended you in some way."

"At least you must let me drive you home," Vernon said, more practically. "It looks like rain."

"That's very kind of you." It *did* look like rain.

"Well, wait a minute and I'll come, too." Lydia seemed curiously reluctant to lose their company.

"Fine idea," Vernon agreed heartily. "Get your coat."

Karen and Jill exchanged glances of not-quite-mock despair as Lydia turned away. Vernon was already jangling his car keys impatiently.

"Why don't we all stop and have a nightcap at that cute little old pub just outside town? You know the one I mean." Lydia came back, buttoning her raincoat.

"It's not far out of our way and it's still so early. Why, it isn't ten o'clock—"

"I really *would* like to get home—" Karen began.

At the same moment, Jill said, "I'm very tired. We've been working devilishly hard all day at the office—"

"Slave-driving again, Vernon?" Lydia gave a light laugh. "I declare, I've *told* you before not to exhaust our guests before they even arrived here. You and your old office—"

The telephone rang abruptly, startling them all. The sudden tense expectancy that whiplashed through a quick look between Lydia and Vernon jolted Karen into a stiff wariness. They were waiting for something, had been waiting all evening.

Was that why she had been brought here tonight? Why they had tried to delay her departure? Were they expecting a telephone call from John? Was he to call them to try to arrange some sort of deal? And was she to be put on the phone to talk to him instead, to try to persuade him to give himself up?

With firm unhurried tread, Vernon crossed to the telephone, frowning slightly. "Vernon Vandergreit here," he said, his tone challenging anyone to deny it.

After that, there was a long silence while Vernon listened, frown deepening, to the person on the other end of the line.

"I'm not sure I understand you—" Finally Vernon spoke again, in a boardroom voice designed to bring unruly subordinates to order. "I can't see what—"

From the incredulous expression on his face, the person at the other end had had the temerity to cut him off sharply. Once again he listened in silence.

"Yes . . ." Now Vernon spoke very slowly, the frown seemed in danger of becoming a permanent fixture. "Yes, that *is* the number of—" He glanced across the room and stopped abruptly.

"Yes . . ." His voice was even quieter, cautious. "Yes, I think that *would* be best. No, that won't be necessary. My car is right outside. I can be there in a few minutes . . . Not at all." He replaced the receiver solemnly and seemed to brace himself before looking up to meet the combined gaze of the waiting women.

"Vernon," Lydia began, "what on earth—?"

"I'm sorry, dear, I have to go out for a while." The warning shake of his head was faint but unmistakable. "Why don't you call a taxi and take our guests—"

"That won't be necessary," Karen said. "We can walk there in the time we'd spend waiting for a taxi." She hoped that Lydia wouldn't offer to walk with them.

"Yes," Jill seconded, crowding her briskly towards the door. "We must get back. I'm exhausted and—"

"But, Vernon," Lydia wailed. "They *can't* go yet."

The door began to swing shut behind them. It closed on an abruptly-harsh raised voice they hardly recognized as Vernon's.

"It doesn't matter now!" Vernon said.

Walking the short distance home, they were both silent. By tacit consent, they walked swiftly, impelled by some urgency they could not—or would not—put a name to.

A light was burning in the house as they neared it and Jill halted abruptly, turning to Karen.

"No," Karen said. "I know who it is."

Silently again, they approached the house and the door swung open as they came up the path.

"I got through earlier than I expected," Ian Feltham said. "I've been making myself at home. I hope you don't mind." The last was an afterthought, he didn't care whether she minded or not.

Karen murmured something polite, not missing the quick flicker of interest in Jill's eyes. Dully she registered that Ian Feltham was an attractive man, one who might be considered eligible in other circumstances. But Jill didn't know about the circumstances—

Jill's glance turned to her, speculative now, and Karen was conscious with a small shock of apprehension that Jill was on the verge of suspecting her. Of what, probably not even Jill was sure yet.

Karen had a sensation of losing ground, of seeing a life-long ally in danger of slipping away. Could Jill really imagine that she had already begun to console herself in John's absence? Worse, might Jill think that something had been going on for a longer period of time? That perhaps it was the real reason behind John's defection? It was time to clear the air.

"Jill, this is Dr. Feltham. Ian Feltham—Grace's fiancé."

"Oh!" Jill rallied quickly and smiled, extending her hand automatically. "How do you do?"

"Not very well at the moment." He took her hand briefly and released it, turning to Karen. "I saw the light you left on for me and so I—"

"But I didn't leave a light on," Karen said. "I never do."

"Never?" His tone was disbelieving, he looked beyond her, his gaze probing the farthest corners of the room. "Perhaps you forgot to turn it off when you left the house. You were in a hurry and—"

"I didn't *have* a light on. It was still broad daylight when I left the house." She, too, had begun looking around the room warily.

"See here—" Jill sensibly put it into words. "Why don't we just take a look through the house? It may sound silly, but I'd be a lot happier if we even looked under the beds. We're alone here in the house—or we will be when Dr. Feltham leaves."

"I'd be happier, too," he said. "I don't like the idea of an intruder—"

While he had been speaking, Karen had been moving towards the studio door. Now she threw it open, snapping on the light. The studio was empty, but the protective coverings over the tea service and the chess set were wrinkled and awry, as though they had been pulled off and then tossed back hastily, perhaps when the intruder heard Ian Feltham entering the house.

She lifted off the covers herself and checked. It did not seem as though any of the pieces had been disarranged. A quick look must have been as much as the intruder had taken before losing interest—or being interrupted.

"Anything missing?" Ian Feltham was right behind her. Jill lingered in the doorway, keeping watch on both the studio and the living-room.

"No." She replaced the covers, straightening them carefully. "Not from here—"

"And the rest of the house?" He whirled and started for the stairs, Jill following in his wake. Neither glanced back to see if she were with them.

Karen let them go. Jill would be able to tell as well as she if anything important were gone. She doubted that anything of value had been removed—at least, nothing that she had been aware of possessing.

Thoughtfully, she returned to the living-room and sank down into the wing chair, vaguely aware of the distant sounds of search from the upper regions of the house. It seemed pointless, the intruder was not in the house now. Whether he might return at a later time was another matter. But there was no practical way to insure themselves against that eventuality.

First Grace's flat, and now her own home. What were they looking for? The obvious answer was the bearer bonds. But that meant that there was someone else who did not believe that John had taken them. At least, not that he had taken them out of the country with him. But, in that case, why should he have taken them at all? And why should the intruder—

Unless the intruder had been John himself. Unless he

knew that Grace had taken them, intending to throw suspicion upon him because he had access to them. If he had found that out—But that didn't explain why Grace presumably had not had them with her. If she had left them hidden in her own flat, why had she not returned to reclaim them? And if she had not hidden them in her own flat, why on earth should anyone think that she had hidden them here? Grace had rarely visited the house, usually only in connection with business. The last time had been weeks ago. The last time that Karen was aware of. There was nothing to say that Grace had not come back alone at some time when the house was empty and hidden anything she pleased somewhere within its environs. It was becoming increasingly clear that the house was not at all difficult to gain entry to.

A sudden sharp squeal from Jill brought her sitting upright. Then came the sound of footsteps rushing down the stairs, and two voices, both babbling incoherent apologies.

"Terribly sorry—I didn't see your hand there—"

"No, no, it was my fault. I should have moved in time. I didn't realize you were going to close the door—"

They came into the room, Jill with tears standing in her eyes, nursing one hand inside the other.

"Let me take a look at that." Ian Feltham reached for Jill's hand.

"No, really," she drew back. "It's all right—"

"The skin is broken—"

"Some cold water and—"

"Nonsense, I'll get my case. I left it in the car."

"You needn't bother. It will be all right in a minute."

"I don't blame you for hesitating." He grinned wryly. "But I assure you I'm a better doctor than searcher of houses."

"Neither of us is very expert at that." Jill, too, smiled wryly. "It isn't a talent I've ever felt any need to develop."

"Sit down. I'll get my case." He disappeared through the french windows.

"Sorry," Jill glanced up at Karen, who had risen and come to stand over her. "I'm afraid we botched that up pretty badly. But I don't think there is anyone in the house. Not now."

"No," Karen said. "I don't believe there is. I think he slipped away when he heard Ian drive up."

"Yes." Jill stared absently at the thin ridge of blood forming along the back of her hand. "That must be what happened. But who—?"

"That's the question, isn't it?" Their eyes met gravely. "If we knew that—"

"You don't suppose it *could* be—?" Jill broke off and looked away. "I mean, if—for some good reason—"

"Some good reason!" Karen was abruptly aware that her short laugh was too high and too shrill, too near the edge of hysteria. She pulled herself back sharply.

"I know we keep saying that," Jill was nervously apologetic. "But there *must* be. If—Oh, I don't know—" She broke off, wincing. In her earnestness, she had gripped her own injured hand too hard. "Ow!"

"It's a nightmare," Karen agreed. "And I can't wake up. I keep trying to, but I can't. Every time I go to sleep, I think that perhaps this time I'll finish the horrible dream and be free of it. Then I wake up and it's still there."

In the distance, they heard a car door slam. Karen drew herself up and retreated to the wing chair. For some inexplicable reason she did not feel that she wanted Ian Feltham to find her holding any sort of unofficial conference with Jill. Perhaps because he might be too ready to suspect a conspiracy? She sat down in the wing chair trying to look as though she had never stirred from it.

Jill stared across at her. "I don't know what to say. I can't think of anything helpful—or hopeful. I suppose one day we'll look back on all this and—"

"Don't tell me we'll call it 'the good old days'." Once again her abortive laugh was too shrill and unsteady.

"No," Jill said. "I wouldn't tell you that."

The silence gathered between them then. Karen felt that they were both listening for Ian's footsteps, waiting for him to return and pull them back from the dangerous precipice they had strayed too close to.

Instead, the telephone rang.

"Karen? Good, you're still up." Vernon Vandergreit's voice was barely recognizable, it sounded strained and odd. "You're going to be up for a while longer, aren't you? I mean, you aren't going to bed early? We thought we might drop over for a while."

"Vernon—*now*?" This was too much—and she had no compunction about letting it show in her tone.

"I know it's late, but there's something we've got to talk about—"

"Vernon, we've been together and talking all evening. If you haven't said everything by now, surely whatever's left can wait until morning."

"Karen—" If it hadn't been Vernon, the voice might

almost have been pleading. "Morning may be too late."

"Too late?" Abruptly, alarm flooded her mind. "Vernon, what is it? Have you heard from John?"

"No . . ." Vernon said slowly. "That is, I don't *think* so. Not directly—"

"Vernon—"

"We've got to discuss it now, do you see?" Vernon said urgently. "We've got to decide what line we're going to take and all agree to stick to it—no matter what."

Get our stories straight, he meant. And there would be only one reason for doing that.

"Vernon, do you mean you're going to call in the police?" It was time, it was more than time. It was what she had been pressing for since John's disappearance first became known. Yet now she felt a curious reluctance to have it happen.

"Not exactly." Vernon sighed. "I'm afraid the police are already involved. *They* called *me*. That was why I couldn't drive you home. I had to go to the police station."

"Vernon, what's happened?" She could scream, she could shake him! That low, slow, ponderous voice, endlessly going on, yet never coming to the point, never willing to divulge any solid information. "*Tell* me."

"Steady." She was dimly aware that Jill had moved to stand supportively behind her and was listening, too.

"I suppose you'll have to know, Karen, sooner or later." He paused reluctantly.

"Yes, Vernon." She tried to control her voice. "Obviously I will. And I'd prefer to know sooner."

"They've found the company car. They traced the registration to us.'' Having brought himself to the point of telling her, his voice was so loud—almost defiant—that she had to hold the receiver a little distance away from her ear. Even so, his voice resounded loudly.

''They pulled the company car out of Millrace Pond late this afternoon. Grace—Grace's body was in it.''

''And John?'' she gasped faintly.

''We'll be there in ten minutes,'' he said firmly. ''We can discuss it then.'' There was a decisive click.

''Vernon—Vernon!''

Then Jill was prying the receiver from her hand, murmuring something she paid no attention to. She raised her head and looked across the room to see Ian Feltham standing just inside the french windows. He looked stricken.

With a mixture of dismay and relief, she realized that he must have heard Vernon's announcement. She would not have to break the news to him herself.

CHAPTER 14

"**T**HIS is a terrible thing," Harvey said. "Terrible." He looked around the room earnestly, but avoided meeting Karen's eyes. There was nothing unusual about that. No one had even looked directly at her, far less into her eyes, since they had all arrived.

"No one is disputing that, Har-vee." Simone flicked him an impatient glance. She seemed to be deeply occupied with thoughts of her own—more probably, calculations.

Derek had been pouring and handing round drinks. Not even Lydia had felt able to suggest coffee this time. Now he poured a final drink for himself and perched on the edge of a chair, ready to move again the instant he got a signal for a fresh drink from anyone. Apart from accepting a drink, Simone still appeared to be ignoring him.

"Now, the way I see it—" Vernon Vandergreit had reassumed his Boardroom manner. "We need only deal with the immediate problem. I mean, we don't want to cloud the issue by dragging in any extraneous details when the police question us. *If* they question us—and I don't really see why they should—they're only going to be interested in Grace. We want to keep our answers short and to the point. We don't want to volunteer any information they're not aware of.''

In other words, we don't mention John, bearer bonds or embezzlement.

"Grace was not a happy woman," Lydia said tentatively. She seemed to be trying out the words to decide how she liked the sound of them. "I always felt there was something unsettled . . . disturbed . . . about her. I can't say I'm surprised at this development.''

"She was worried about her job," Harvey embroidered upon the theme. "We're in the midst of a pretty thoroughgoing reorganization here. There was going to be no room for dead wood—and she knew it.''

"I wouldn't call her work outstanding." Derek seemed hesitant about his contribution. He offered it diffidently and looked around for approval.

"Grace was not a happy woman." Ignoring him, Simone picked up the refrain smoothly. "She was not especially young, she was not pretty. She had nothing but her job and—''

"We try to be fair." Vernon Vandergreit shook his head slowly. "But we are in an expansive, go-ahead cycle and some people just don't have what it takes to keep up with the others. It's very unfortunate but, for the good of the company, these changes have to be made. I'm afraid Grace was smart enough to see what was coming—''

"The handwriting on the wall," Lydia said. "And she simply couldn't face it, poor thing.''

It was smooth, effortless, inexorable. Even as they

talked, they were moving from rehearsal to full performance, convincing each other, convincing themselves. As they would convince anyone who questioned them in the morning. There were just a few little snags, but they weren't aware of those yet.

Beside her, Karen heard the sharp intake of Ian Feltham's breath and braced herself for the explosion which was to come. Meanwhile, the others continued unheedingly, trying out their case, bringing in their verdict.

"This is a tragic thing," Harvey said. "Tragic. We've never had a suicide in Vandergreit Enterprises before."

"Poor, poor creature," Lydia said. "If only she could have reached out to one of us for help. If only we had had any idea—"

"We could have done nothing," Simone said. "Women like Grace—their job is their whole life. They have nothing else. It is most symbolic that she should have used the company car to accomplish her fate. She felt the need to have something representing her job and her security with her to the very end." She bowed her head sadly to the fitness of Grace's choice.

"Yes, it all falls into place," Vernon agreed. "Especially when—just between ourselves—we consider the background. But I should hope that some of the other little problems we've been having at Harding Handicrafts can be kept from the attention of the police and public." He slanted a cautious look at Karen, evidently expecting her to leap on any bandwagon which promised to exonerate her husband, to throw all the blame on to the shoulders of a dead woman who could not defend herself.

Karen returned his gaze steadily, keeping silent. After a moment, he looked away uneasily.

"We must consider our liabilities," Simone said crisply, raising her head. "I assume this is to say that the company car is a complete write-off?"

"Oh, that sounds so *cold*," Lydia wailed. "Don't put it like that. Can't we just be glad that it was some kind of comfort to her when she had nothing else—nothing of her own? It must have meant something very special to her for her to use it for her suicide like that."

"It wasn't suicide!"

Ian Feltham's voice had not been raised before. The others turned to him, startled. They had been paying no attention to him. Obviously they had assumed, if they bothered to consider his presence at all, that he was there because Karen was his patient. They had not expected him to contribute anything to the meeting, far less a judgement.

"I beg your pardon." Vernon's tone indicated that he did no such thing. "Did I understand you to say—"

"It wasn't suicide." His voice was lower, calmer now—but cold, deadly cold. "Grace had no reason to commit suicide."

"But we have just been telling you—" Something in his face stopped Simone abruptly. She lowered her eyelids and watched him warily through narrow slits that veiled any expression.

A new tenseness invaded the room. Nerves that had been relaxing and expanding under the autohypnosis of their own hypocrisy suddenly snapped taut again. An unknown quantity had appeared amongst them. They waited to see how much of a danger he would be.

"Grace was not worried about losing her job. She was good at it and in no danger of losing it. In fact, she was in line for a promotion—and I believe most of you knew it."

Guarded silence. Perhaps guilty, but the Board members were well accustomed to masking guilt until, in their own deliberations, they produced enough mass justification to turn it into innocence, turn themselves into the injured parties. They continued waiting.

"Even if Grace *had* lost her job—" he looked from face to face, challenging them as he demolished their arguments—"it wouldn't have been the end of the world for her. It would just have meant a rearrangement of her plans—*our* plans."

No muscle moved in the watching faces. It was as though they all knew what he was about to say now, were braced for it, and were already thinking of ways in which to refute it.

"We were engaged to be married."

No one showed any sign of surprise. Rather, there was a feeling in the air of intense mental activity. Ideas were rapidly being revised, stories being amended to encompass this new discovery.

"Grace was ambitious. Because she was hoping for promotion, we'd delayed the wedding. But if she had lost her job, we would have married immediately, perhaps have started a family—" He broke off, swallowed, and concluded. "So, you see, no matter what happened at Harding Handicrafts, it wouldn't have been the end of the world for her. She had no reason whatsoever to commit suicide."

The silence in the room lengthened until Vernon Vandergreit cleared his throat and moved uneasily.

"An accident, then," he said. "That must be the explanation. Grace had taken the car—and it's a big car, bigger than a woman would be used to handling—"

"Grace couldn't drive!"

A quiver of annoyance ran through the room. They assimilated this information in silence again.

"Are you positive about that?" Harvey asked slowly. "It does seem to me that I always had the impression that she could drive. Not that she was a good driver, perhaps, or even a very frequent one—but I could have sworn that she drove."

"No." He was firm, definite, but the balance of power in the room was subtly shifting again. Silent messages were exchanged, eyes met and slid away, heads nodded imperceptibly.

"But you are wrong!" Simone was as definite as he. "Grace was learning to drive. I have given her a lesson myself."

"There now," Harvey said. "That would explain the impression I had. Of course she wasn't a very good driver as she was just learning. But I was certain she could drive."

"That's it!" Lydia sighed with satisfaction. "That explains everything. Grace *could* drive—a little bit. And you didn't know it because she was just learning to." Lydia fixed Ian Feltham with a limpid gaze. "Probably she was planning to surprise you."

"She never mentioned such a thing—" For the first time, Ian Feltham sounded uncertain.

"Well, she wouldn't, if she wanted it to be a surprise, would she?" Lydia smiled gently. "She'd want to wait until she got her licence and then just drive up and say, 'Look at me—I'm driving!' That's the only way a surprise is really good. Of course, she wouldn't tell you about it before-hand—then you'd *know*."

"Derek, too, has given Grace lessons," Simone prompted. There was an unenthusiastic dryness in her tone which fleetingly made one wonder just what sort of lessons Derek had given.

"That's right," Derek said eagerly. His eyes turned to Simone, begging for approval. "Several times. She—She was anxious to learn—but she wasn't a good driver. She'd never be that. She couldn't possibly have handled a car as powerful as the company car. I don't know what possessed her to try. It was asking for trouble—"

"The forbidden has its own fascination," Simone said. "The forbidden, the unattainable and the uncontrollable. This is well known. Grace would have felt the challenge."

"That's true." Vernon Vandergreit moved in on cue. They were all operating as a team again, smooth, efficient—implacable.

"An accident." Vernon handed down the verdict decisively. "A tragic, sad accident. A young woman with a brilliant career ahead of her, a fine marriage in the offing, everything to live for—and then the vagaries of Fate stepped in. An automobile accident."

The tune had certainly changed from the original rendition, but the others had taken up the chorus without missing a beat. There was only one discordant note.

"I don't believe it!" Ian Feltham said.

"Don't be silly," Lydia said softly. "If it wasn't suicide, then it must have been an accident. What else could it be?"

"I don't believe it either," Karen said. It was the first time she had spoken in so long that the others stared at her as though a marble statue had suddenly given voice.

"What else could it be?" Lydia repeated.

"Misadventure," Derek offered quickly. "That's the sort of thing officials always decide—misadventure."

He meant coroners. The thought shouldn't have come with such a shock. It was part of the natural progression of events. The police didn't just pull a drowned body in a car out of Millrace Pond and say, "Tut, tut, these things will happen." There would be an enquiry, an inquest, to find out what had happened. They would want to know the background, the people involved—if possible, the reasons for the event.

That was what this meeting was all about. That was why everyone wanted their story straight before morning when the official questioning would begin.

"Misadventure," Derek insisted. "That's the best we can try for." He looked about for support—even to Simone.

"Mis-adven-ture." Simone tasted the word slowly and nodded. "That might be the best solution."

"Misadventure." Vernon weighed in decisively. "That would explain everything."

"Not quite everything," Ian Feltham said. He looked around the room, letting them see that he knew the whole story, the background they were hoping to conceal. "In fact, I'd say it explains nothing. Nothing pertinent." He challenged Karen directly. "Would *you* be satisfied with that explanation?"

She hesitated.

"What *else* could it be?" Lydia's voice was soft and insinuating, her eyes too wise, threatening an answer that was unthinkable.

"She is right," Simone said. "If you do not like suicide, if you are not content with accident, or with misadventure—then what remains?"

Murder! John! Karen shook her head blindly, denying it. Beside her, Jill stirred restlessly.

111

"You see." Simone, watching intently, pressed home their advantage. "Is not misadventure preferable to that?"

"Not to *me*!" It was an open declaration of war from Ian Feltham. His eyes were hostile, their brief partisanship dissolved under the impact of the knowledge that Grace was dead. She could not blame him. That changed everything for him—and for her, too. "I want to know the truth."

"There are many truths." Simone shrugged. "The wise man accepts the truth which is most acceptable. I think it would be better if you were wise."

"Better for whom?"

"Better for all concerned." Vernon frowned meaningly towards Karen, evidently unable or unwilling to believe that she was not Ian Feltham's patient, and thus someone whose interests he might be concerned in protecting.

"Oh?" Ian turned to look at her, his eyes searching her face curiously. Did he suspect her of complicity? From the first, he had shown signs of not being completely sure that her interests were not those of either the Company or her defaulting husband. He now had a right to be more dubious than ever.

"It isn't true," Karen said, speaking only to him. "We both know that."

"Do we?" He followed her more closely than the others, who still thought that they were talking about a verdict on Grace.

"You must understand, Kaa-ren, that it is not to *anyone's* advantage that Grace's death leads to an investigation of Company affairs," Simone began.

"How do we know that?" He cut across Simone, glaring at Karen. "If your husband has absconded with the Company funds, murdering my fiancée in the process, then why shouldn't the police know about it? Why shouldn't the whole bloody world know about it?''

''You're upset, poor boy.'' Lydia switched to womanly sympathy. ''This is terrible for you, we understand that. But you really shouldn't speak to poor Karen like that. She's going through a difficult time, too, you know.''

It wasn't up to Lydia's usual standard. They were all thrown off course by this unexpected obstacle in their path. Behind the bland faces, brains were busily working, trying to discover some means of attaining ascendancy over the unknown quantity, of enlisting him on their side.

''John is *not* a murderer!''

''Of course not—'' ''No, no—'' ''Unthinkable—'' Harvey, Simone and Derek all started to speak at once, then stopped and babbled apologies to each other.

Karen and Ian exchanged glances, briefly reunited in annoyance. There were things to be decided—fought out, if you like—and they could neither fight nor make decisions in front of this unwanted audience.

How could she be rid of them? She wished she had the courage simply to order them out of the house. ''*Stand not upon the order of your going*—'' But she could not do that—they were trying to help, they wanted to be kind.

Why couldn't they realize that the situation had now gone beyond the point where anything could help? Not kindness, not misguided support, least of all their presence. Nothing.

Except finding out what had happened. Except knowing for certain whether or not John was still alive.

''Are they *sure* that Grace was alone in the car?'' she asked desperately.

''She was alone.'' Simone was positive. ''And the car

doors were closed. It was not as though one door was swinging open so that—'' She stopped abruptly.

So that a body could have fallen out.

''In any case,'' Derek said helpfully, ''the police are dragging the pond. If there's anything in there, they'll find—'' He intercepted a poisonous glare from Simone and stopped short.

Everything blurred. One moment the room had been bright, every face sharp and clear. Then, as though a sudden fog had invaded the room, everything was blurred—even voices—and distant. She was not aware that she had fallen back against the chair. She felt a hand grasping her wrist and only vaguely identified fingers being pressed firmly against vein and artery.

''That's all for tonight, I think,'' Ian Feltham ordered.

The mists were clearing already. It had only been a momentary weakness, but she kept her eyes closed, realizing that her purpose was being achieved. The others were leaving.

Still in the distance, she heard Jill speeding the parting guests with proper-sounding hostess noises, quite as though they had been invited and this had been a normal social gathering.

She heard, too, Ian Feltham's voice saying, ''Just a moment, please.''

She opened her eyes a cat's slit seeing that, with unerring instinct, he had discerned the weakest link in the chain. His hand was on Derek Conway's arm, and he had drawn Derek back into the room.

''Just one question,'' Ian said. ''I'm sorry to delay you, but the climate seems a bit too emotional where the others are concerned. I thought I could get a calmer, more reasoned answer from you.''

''Oh. Well, I'll try.'' Derek could never resist flattery—it was written in the weak blink of his eyes, in the impeccable creases of his suit—and Ian Feltham had read the signs correctly. Derek gave a man-to-man nod. ''Naturally, the others are quite upset. You can't blame them.''

''No, of course not,'' Ian soothed expertly. ''This whole episode has been quite appalling.''

And it's not over yet. Incredulously, Karen watched Derek preen, assuming the cloak he had long coveted—that of one of the Board of Directors. He had forgotten—or overlooked—the fact that Ian Feltham was intimately concerned in the problem. Perhaps he subscribed so thoroughly to Simone's fiction that he still thought of Grace as a lone and friendless woman on the verge of losing the job which was her only reason for living. Certainly he seemed to have no realization that he was speaking to her recently-bereaved fiancé.

''Appalling, yes,'' Derek agreed, unconsciously adopting the portentous tones of Vernon Vandergreit. ''And at a time like this. It could ruin everything.''

''Everything?'' Ian asked sympathetically, a trace of asperity sounding through before he carefully modified his tone. ''But not irrevocably, surely?'' The conscious blandness in his voice was offset sharply by the spark glinting in his eyes. ''Not irretrievably?''

''It could be, old chap.'' Derek shook his head. ''If this isn't hushed up, it could set all our plans back two or three years—if not dish them altogether.''

''I mean—'' he appealed for even more sympathy—''how could we go public with a scandal like this hanging over us?''

CHAPTER 15

*G*OING *Public. So that was it.*

That was the reason for the excessive concern of the Board of Directors. It had nothing to do with loyalty to John, nor with any belief in his innocence. They were simply worried about concealing the situation in order that their reputation could be maintained, so that a share issue could be floated and subscribed without any suspicion on the part of Stock Exchange or public that there was anything murky beneath the calm and sunny waters of Harding Handicrafts.

That was why they were working so hard to pass Grace's death off as an isolated incident. Something that must in no way be connected with any other unusual happenings in the vicinity of Harding Handicrafts. Grace had just had an unfortunate accident—a misadventure. Their General Manager was simply a bit overdue back from a business trip to the Continent and had foolishly neglected to notify either the company or his wife. *Boys will be boys and everything's lovely in the garden.*

But could the auditors be persuaded to agree to such a misrepresentation of facts? Could they be suborned by the smiles, the lies, the evasions? Or would they take a bribe? Who chose the auditors? How honest were they? Or were they chosen because it was known that they were susceptible to a little discreet corruption?

"Actually—" Derek had lowered his voice which, in some perverse way, ensured that it carried more clearly than before—"it may be even worse than we know at the moment."

Karen moved infinitesimally, settling farther back into the sheltering shadows of the wing chair as Derek glanced warily in her direction.

"There are discrepancies in some of the accounts." Reassured, Derek continued. "Simone began finding them some weeks ago. We've managed to conceal them from the auditors so far, but—"

"Derek, we are awaiting you!" Whip-sharp, Simone's voice slashed across his revelations. She stood in the doorway with the face of an avenging fury. Behind her, Jill hovered nervously.

"Yes, yes. I'm coming." Derek deflated abruptly. He gave Ian an apologetic smile and began edging towards the doorway.

"Sorry." Ian relinquished his hold on Derek's arm reluctantly, watching him escape just as he was becoming informative. "Perhaps I can talk to you again. Tomorrow? You'll be in your office?"

"Yes, if you like." The others were massed just beyond

the doorway, waiting to reclaim the strayed lamb. "Yes, I'll be there. If you think it's important—?"

How much had they heard? Every face looked grim and set.

"Not vitally important, no." Ian sent an easy smile towards the intent faces. "But I must admit that what you've said puts a different aspect on some of Grace's most recent attitudes." His voice beamed out reassuringly. "You've almost persuaded me that she *could* have had an accident, after all."

Or a misadventure. But the waiting faces had relaxed, were regarding Derek with a warmth that was close to approval. If he had succeeded where they had failed, they would be willing to forgive him much. And, with Derek, there was always much to forgive.

"Come, then—" Even Simone's voice was more cordial, her expression less jaundiced. "We are all tired. Kaaren must be allowed some sleep before she collapses. It will not do if she is unable to speak to the authorities should she be called upon to do so. She must rest and be strong for the morning—although it is unlikely that they will think to disturb her."

"She'll be all right, won't she?" Lydia appealed to Jill. "If there's anything at all we can do—If you'd like me to stay the night? You need some rest yourself. And you must want to get back to London some time and take care of your own concerns."

"Not at all." Jill spoke hastily. "I've arranged things so that I can stay as long as Karen needs me. And I can sleep just as well here as at my own flat. We can manage, thank you, by ourselves."

More truthful than tactful, perhaps, but Lydia did not seem unduly put off. "Well, if there *is* anything at all I can do, you just let me know, y'hear?"

"I hear," Jill said. "I mean, I will. And thank you. I appreciate that—we both appreciate it." The hour was late, they were all close to exhaustion, the distaste in Jill's voice was thinly concealed.

"Well, mind that you do—" Then, thankfully, Vernon's hand was at Lydia's elbow, piloting her out into the night.

"We've got quite a lot to do tomorrow." Harvey lingered, speaking to Jill. "If you *could* get to the office a bit early—"

Poor Harvey, he always threw himself into his work with extra vigour when Olive was back in the States. It was as though he had to prove to himself that the good of the company depended upon him remaining here and working unstintingly while those less conscientious took it easy.

"Yes, I will," Jill promised recklessly. Anything to get him out of the house. Her relief was palpable as he turned and walked away after a long moment of projecting what was evidently intended to be a meaning look into her eyes.

Karen heard the car doors slam and the motors start up before she moved. Jill and Ian were in murmured consultation by the french windows. They stopped murmuring and turned their heads as she stood up.

"You're better." Jill started forward.

"You can't believe John had anything to do with Grace's death!" Bypassing Jill, she attacked Ian directly.

"Then where is he?"

"I don't know." She slumped back into the chair, aware that she had begun to tremble. "All I can think is that he must be dead, too. I don't want to believe it—but there's no other answer. While they're dragging the pond, perhaps they'll find—'' She closed her eyes, trying to shut out the images that rose before her.

"Don't think about it," Jill said quickly. "Not any more tonight. In the morning—"

Things will seem better? Karen opened her eyes and Jill flinched at the look in them.

"John isn't a thief." Karen turned back to Ian. "And he isn't a murderer."

"Then how did Grace get into that pond? Do *you* believe she'd been taking driving lessons?" His mouth twisted. "Do you believe any of *them* were teaching her to drive?"

"No." It all came back to this—the blank wall of what had been going on behind the scenes at Harding Handicrafts. What had been the real relationships between these people? *Could* any of the things they had been insinuating about John and Grace really have been true?

If they had, then she had never really known him herself. Their entire life together had been a lie, a facade behind which he had lived a private life of his own, a life in which she had no part.

"Grace isn't—wasn't—a thief, either," Ian Feltham said. Suddenly it occurred to her that he must be ravaged by the same doubts and questions as she. "Nor would she have committed suicide. And accident—or misadventure—" his mouth twisted again—"is just too pat. I don't believe one damned word of it."

"Neither do I." Jill frowned at both of them. "There's too much about this that doesn't add up."

"None of it does!" He turned to Karen, almost savagely. "What's been going on? That's what I want to know."

"So do I!" She faced him angrily. "Perhaps Grace *had* been taking driving lessons. Perhaps she *did* take the missing bonds and was making her getaway when the car went out of control and into the pond. Perhaps—"

For a moment she thought he was going to strike her. The dangerous flare in his eyes warned her and she stepped back involuntarily.

"This sort of thing won't get us anywhere," Jill intervened smoothly.

"You're right." Ian Feltham checked himself and forced a smile. "We're all overwrought—not surprisingly."

"We certainly are." Jill associated herself with the statement blandly, although she had been the least affected all evening. In fact, she had seemed so far removed from the proceedings at times that she might have been in a theatre watching a cast of actors giving a professional performance. But then, the Board of Harding Handicrafts were very close to being just that. By morning, their act should be polished and nearly perfect.

"I frightened away someone searching the house when I arrived," Ian reminded them. "That must mean there's something to be found."

"Somewhere, not necessarily here," Karen said, thinking of Grace's flat. Thinking, too, that they had only Ian's word for it that there had been an intruder. Perhaps *he* had done the searching himself. She looked up, met his thoughtful gaze and realized that he, too, must be thinking along the same line. *He* had only *her* word for it that Grace's flat had been searched by someone else.

"In any case, we can't do much tonight." Jill stifled a yawn. "I know *I'll* sleep, but—" She looked from Karen to Ian and lifted an eyebrow.

"You may be right." He regarded Karen with a professional eye, the suspicion dying out of it for a moment. "Have you anything to help you sleep?"

"I don't want anything."

"It's not what you want, it's what you need. You're probably too keyed-up tonight to sleep unaided." He pulled a phial from his pocket. "You'd better have a couple of these—I take them myself occasionally."

"I don't—" She caught Jill's eye and fell silent, allowing him to shake two tablets into her hand. Jill needed sleep herself, but would try to stay awake if she thought Karen was not sleeping and might need moral support.

"I'll make a cup of tea," Jill said thankfully, "and then we can get to bed."

"None for me, thanks." Ian replaced the cap on the phial and put it in his pocket. "I've got to get along. I'll ring you in the morning—" He seemed to recall what morning would bring. "When I get a chance," he amended.

"Perhaps I'll see you at the office," Jill offered. "I'll be over there all day again, I suppose. And you're going to talk to Derek at some point. We could go for coffee—" Her face was too bright, too eager. It brought dismay to Karen's heart.

*Oh no! No, Jill—not him, not now. This is no time—*But did love ever choose a time and a place to happen? For a moment her own anguish was swamped in the anguish that might be waiting for Jill, about to love so unwisely, so inopportunely, a man so sunk in his own grief that he could not even see her as a woman at this point in his life.

"If you're not too busy." He was absently civil, unaware of Jill's too-warm smile, too-brilliant eyes. Of course, a stranger would not have realized that her expression was in any way unusual. Perhaps he thought she was as cordial to everyone.

"They *do* let me have time off for coffee breaks." Jill walked to the french windows with him and Karen took the opportunity to slip the unwanted tablets into a pocket.

There were a few more murmured words Karen couldn't quite catch. Something to do with her, obviously. A question—or instructions—before Ian left and Jill turned back into the room.

"I'll make tea now," she said brightly, "and bring you a glass of water so that you can take your sleeping pills."

In dumb show, Karen held out her empty hands and smiled. Not quite a lie. She hadn't said anything, and if Jill chose to believe—

"Taken them already? And without water?" Jill shook her head. "You could always do that—even with aspirins. I never could—they always dissolved in my mouth before I could choke them down—and I loathed the taste. Just tea, then."

"Not for me, thanks." Karen followed her into the kitchen. "I just want some water." She filled a large glass pitcher while Jill watched bemused.

"Are you that thirsty?"

"No." Karen smiled wanly. "It's not for me, it's for my clay. I thought I'd mix a new batch tonight and perhaps do some work—"

"You'll be asleep before you've mixed the clay."

"Then it will be ready for me in the morning." Karen picked up the pitcher and started back for the studio, but paused as she saw Jill make a slight movement, as though to come with her.

"Good night," Karen said firmly. "Sleep well."

"Yes. You, too." Jill hesitated. "And don't worry—No, that's a silly thing to say, isn't it? Just . . . sleep." She turned back to the stove.

Karen carried the pitcher carefully into the studio and set it down on her workbench. She would start the clay in the electric blunger and let it mix while she packed the test kiln.

The tea service and most of the chess set were ready for the first firing. Then she would glaze them and give them their second firing. Finally, apply the coloured glazes and give them the final firing—after which, she would allow Vernon and Lydia to see the finished pieces.

She knelt at the store cupboard John had made for her in the space beneath the window seat and pulled out the bag of clay powder she was using. She carried it over to the workbench and looked at it critically. There wasn't really quite enough powder left. She returned to the window seat and knelt again. There was another bag of clay powder somewhere underneath here, she was sure of it.

She groped for it in faintly bemused annoyance. It must be there—she could not have used it all without noticing it. She always kept a spare bag in reserve. She hated being without an extra. It was unlikely that she might suddenly be inspired to make something that would use every bit of her clay on hand but, if she ever were, it would certainly happen over a weekend when all the shops were closed. And there was nothing more annoying than not having enough material to finish the job in hand.

Unless it was having the material and not being able to put your hand on it. Head and shoulders into the cupboard, trying to keep her grumbles of annoyance to a minimum lest Jill hear and come in to find out what was going on, she rummaged around for the polythene sack, pushing aside jars of glaze powders. It *had* to be in here somewhere.

At last her hand encountered it in the farthest corner of the cupboard. How could it have got pushed back there? She was nearly certain she had seen it within comfortable reaching distance only last week.

She pulled it forward, out of the cupboard and into the light. There was something odd about it. Dust streaked the bag in a peculiar way along with a dusting of fine clay powder, as though it had been opened. But she had not broached this bag, she was sure. She never opened the reserve one until she was ready to use it.

Nevertheless, the sack opened with suspicious ease, the thin metal strip wound so loosely that it sprang apart at the first few light twists. Usually, she had to have John open the bag for her the first time—or else simply claw at the polythene until she had torn a hole in the top.

She pulled the edges apart and plunged her hand into the powder. She had transferred two handfuls into the blunger when, on the third time, she encountered a sudden resistance. She groped around for the object, pulling it free of the powder and brought it out of the bag.

It was another, smaller polythene bag, wrapped closely around a stiff envelope. Holding it over the blunger, she shook off the excess powder and unwound the polythene.

The envelope was large, somewhat official-looking, and definitely not standard equipment to be found in bags of clay powder. She stared at it hopelessly a moment before opening it, half-knowing what she would find.

Bearer bonds. A quarter of a million pounds' worth, Harvey had said. Yet small enough to fit into this envelope and disappear within a sack of clay powder.

John was the only one who could have taken them. The only one who would have thought to hide them here.

Then she had never really known him.

Carefully, keeping all thought at bay, she replaced the bonds in the envelope, rewound the protective polythene film around it and thrust it back into the bag, deep into the powder. She pulled the edges of the bag together, twisted the sealing wire around it, and carried it back to the store cupboard.

Like John, she pushed it into the farthest corner, as far back as it could go, behind the glaze powders where it had been before. Where no one who was searching for it would be likely to find it. Not unless he had left it there himself.

She closed the cupboard door and straightened up, still keeping her mind blank. She undressed and turned down the covers on the divan. She poured some water from the pitcher into a glass, ignoring the waiting powder in the blunger, and swallowed the two sleeping pills.

In bed, she lay rigid with the concentration of keeping her mind blank. It was not until the last treacherous minute when the pills began to take effect that the thought crept into her mind again.

Then she had never really known him.

CHAPTER 16

SHE did not hear Jill leave in the morning, but subconsciously must have been aware that she had gone. Why else awaken with such a start at the sound of faint but unmistakable noises from the kitchen? Something in her knew that there should have been no one there at this hour.

Still hazy from the after effects of the sleeping pills and the continued effort to keep her thoughts at bay, Karen threw on her robe and started towards the kitchen. At the same time, she was aware of a definitive sound from the kitchen and knew that the intruder was heading in her direction now.

They met in the living-room, Simone carrying a tray. "Ah, Kaa-ren," she said. "You are awake. That is good. I have made your breakfast. Now you can eat it."

"So I see." Karen dropped into the wing chair and stared broodingly at the tray. A pot of coffee, two empty cups, and rather too much toast told her that she was not going to breakfast alone. "How . . . thoughtful of you."

127

"I like to do things for people." Simone set the tray on the coffee table and moved an armchair closer for herself. "In any case, I am wanting to talk to you, and this has seemed the best opportunity. We cannot speak with too many people always around."

More questions. Instantly, guiltily, her mind projected the picture of the sack in the closet with the concealed bearer bonds so vividly that she looked away, half-afraid that the very intensity of the vision might have materialized it on the table between them.

When she glanced back, Simone was complacently pouring coffee, thankfully not a mind-reader. The morning post lay in a small pile beside the sugar bowl. She reached for it, aware that it could contain nothing of interest—nothing from John—or Simone would have mentioned it.

She was aware of Simone's calculating gaze as she shuffled through the envelopes, knowing that what she longed for could not be there, but finding that hope was not abandoned so easily. No familiar handwriting, no foreign postmark. With a faint sigh, she replaced the post on the tray. Time enough to open it later.

"No," Simone sighed in sympathy. "I am meeting the postman as I arrive and I have seen there is nothing there. If there had been, I would have awakened you immediately."

I'll bet you would have. Karen stretched out her hand, accepting the coffee. "Thank you."

"I think you do not pay enough attention." Simone eyed her critically. "I think you have not paid enough attention for a long time now. That is why I wish to speak to you."

"Perhaps not," Karen admitted. Would John have gone off the rails like this if she had been paying enough attention? Could she have noted the beginning of the slide, arrested it, slowed it? Or had it already been too late at some point long before she could have done anything? Would she ever really know? What had gone wrong?

"I've been trying to remember." She locked glances with Simone earnestly. "But, in all honesty, I can't pinpoint any time at which John seemed odd—not normal. He always seemed just the same. I couldn't have had any idea—"

"No, no!" Simone interrupted impatiently. "This is not what I mean. This is in the past now. This is why I say you do not pay enough attention. Even now you do not listen."

"Yes." Karen sipped at her coffee abstractedly. "I *am* listening."

"You do not look as though you are," Simone complained. "And you must because this is important. It is your future I wish to discuss."

The future—do I have one? It sounded like a proposition for a debate. Which side would Simone take—the affirmative or the negative?

"I don't believe I feel like discussing that just now."

"Always you English are so—so secretive!" Simone exploded. "One cannot—"

"I believe you mean reticent." It was below the belt and it was meant to be. She watched Simone flush with anger, but felt unrepentant.

"Very well—reticent." Simone added more sugar to her coffee and stirred with unnecessary vigour. "You do not speak your minds and others do not know what you always mean. It upsets. Lydia and Vernon have been very hurt. This is what I must say to you."

"Lydia and Vernon?" Karen echoed in astonishment. "But—"

"They have shown you every kindness," Simone said severely. "They have tried to help you in the best way they know—and you do not respond. This is not nice, Kaa-ren. This is not even polite."

"Respond?" Whatever she had expected from Simone, it was not this. Guiltily, the picture of the sack of clay powder flashed across her mind again. "I'm afraid I don't understand."

"That is because you do not pay attention! I am explaining to them that you do not mean to be rude, but you do not pay attention, and this is why they are still awaiting your answer. Such an opportunity anyone else would have jumped for."

"Opportunity?" She felt at a complete loss. She was paying attention now, but Simone might as well have been speaking Sanskrit. "I don't know what you're talking about."

"Of course you do not." Simone poured more coffee. "This is because you do not pay—"

"You've made that point," Karen interrupted, with rising annoyance. "Several times. Can we now get on with the subject in hand—whatever it may be."

"Lydia and Vernon think so much of you—of your gifts—and they have always spoken most highly of you. It is not right that you should ignore them like this."

"Ignore them?" *I'd like to get the chance!* Karen thought of all the hours they had been spending together during the past week. "They were here only last night— practically all night. I wouldn't call that ignoring them."

"They have great plans for you which you ignore, ideas you avoid, invitations you do not answer. They are most hurt."

"Invitations?" Lydia had, on several occasions recently, invited *herself* to stay overnight in Karen's home and been repulsed. Was that what Simone was referring to?

"They wish you to return to New York with them," Simone said. "It is an opportunity many would give their teeth for—and you do not even respond."

"New York—at a time like this? You can't mean they were serious."

"Naturally they are serious. Lydia and Vernon do not make jokes where business is concerned. Surely you realize this?"

"Yes, I suppose I do." Abstractedly, Karen allowed Simone to refill her cup. "But I can't consider anything like that right now. They were talking about some time in the future and, in the present circumstances—"

"You are not to blame for anything your husband has done. Lydia and Vernon understand this. This is why they wish to help you to make a new life."

They might wait until I've finished with the old one. But the vision of the hidden bearer bonds rose up before her again. *Had* she finished with the old life? *Or had the old life finished with her?*

"You are upset." Simone interpreted her silence. "This is natural. You do not think ahead. Perhaps you do not think at all. This, too, is natural. This is why you must permit your friends to think and plan for you."

Upset, yes. But was it wise to let "friends" do too much thinking for one? Such friends as wanted to do the most planning were not entirely uninvolved.

"You would like New York," Simone urged. "Lydia and Vernon would take every care of you. They plan that you

131

should live with them until you can find a flat of your own—
and then there would be a bonus that you may furnish it.
There will be a job waiting for you—you will be earning
much money. And Lydia has said that there are many handsome young executives in their American headquarters—''

''My husband has not been gone a week yet,'' Karen said
coldly. ''Don't you think it's a bit soon to plan my re-
marriage?''

''As it may be.'' Simone shrugged. ''But you must start
thinking about it some time. It is best to face facts—''

First Lydia and Vernon, then Harvey, and now Simone.
They were all pushing too hard, trying to force her into
rearranging her life too quickly. Why couldn't they realize
that she needed time to think?

''You must not allow yourself to sit here and brood,''
Simone said. The phrase brought back echoes of Lydia. Of
course, it was an American attitude to equate thinking with
brooding. Action—any kind of action, however aimless—
was preferable to thought.

''It is not even necessary that you make up your mind
immediately. Lydia and Vernon will send you over to the
States now for a holiday. A week or two, and you will see
how much you like it there. And Har-vee's wife, Olive, will
meet you at the airport and take care of you. You will have
nothing to concern yourself with.''

Everyone wants to take care of me. Or did they simply
want to get her out of the way?

''But Olive will be back next month,'' Karen protested.
''They can't mean me to go so soon.''

''For a holiday, yes. I tell you, Kaa-ren, it is ideal.'' Sens-
ing capitulation, Simone pressed harder. ''You will be able to

fly back with her. You will have a holiday among friends, and a travelling companion for your return journey." *What more,* Simone's tone implied, *could one possibly wish?*

"I'll have to think it over," Karen temporized.

"Always this thinking!" Simone exploded. "It is not healthy! Why do you not decide 'Yes' now? You could be on a plane tonight. Or in the morning. A few hours and you are in a new world. Many people would envy you this chance."

"I suppose they would," Karen said, allowing herself to sound tempted.

"It is natural—" Simone launched into a further sales talk, while Karen held an interested look on her face and stopped listening, but began thinking rapidly.

What was going on? First, there had been the sudden passion on everyone's part to take her out and feed her. Was it just coincidence that, returning from one of those dinner parties, she found that her house had been entered and searched? She hardly thought so.

Now she knew that there had been something to find. Which meant that someone else had known that, too. Perhaps had even known what—but not where, since Grace's flat had also been the subject of a thorough-going search. That meant that it could not have been John's doing. He had hidden the bonds and was not likely to have forgotten their hiding place. In any case, he could have returned to the house under cover of darkness with reasonable certitude that she would not immediately hand him over to the police. Not before an explanation. *Was there an explanation?*

"You *need* a holiday at this time," Simone insisted. "Even a week in another country and you will return feeling stronger and better able to bear what must eventually be done."

What must be done? A divorce? Or begin the process of having John declared "Missing, presumed dead?" But that took seven years, didn't it? Or a funeral? But, for that, one had to have a body. Only Grace's body had turned up—so far.

John had hidden the bonds in his own home, which indicated that he had expected to return there. Furthermore, he must have known that his place of concealment would not have been adequate indefinitely. He was nearly as expert as she at judging how long her clay would last. He must have noticed that the opened sack was almost used up. He would have known that it would not be long before she opened the other sack. Therefore, it was reasonable to assume that he had planned to be back before that time. He had either taken a calculated risk that he would be back before then, or he had trusted her to keep quiet about her discovery in case something detained him and he couldn't make it in time.

"You are not paying attention!" Simone accused.

"I am." *Oh yes, I am.* Paying more attention now than perhaps she had ever paid in her life before. Never before had the stakes been quite so high.

"You do not look as though you are."

"Actually, I was wondering what I had to wear. I mean, it will be autumn in New York now. I understand it can be either very hot or very cold there at this time. I was thinking over my wardrobe and—"

"You can buy new clothes there," Simone said triumphantly. "Lydia and Vernon will see that you can have money there. You do not have to worry about the official travel allowance. These things can be arranged."

"I'm sure Lydia and Vernon are expert at such arrangements.'' Fortunately Simone did not suspect irony, she was too pleased at the success of her own machinations.

"But yes! No one is more able at such things. This is natural when they have so much to do with so many foreign countries. They are indeed expert.''

"That's what I thought.'' Karen smiled, trying to look as compliant as they all obviously supposed her to be. That was the way she must appear now: vague, compliant, perhaps still rather distraught. But unsuspicious.

They had tried to get her out of the house—and there had been something to find in it. Now they were trying to get her out of the country. There must still be something to discover, some way in which she could be a danger—even more so than in her insistence that the police must be informed. Something to discover. But what?

Whatever it was, it was not to be found here. Not now. Where then? At Harding Handicrafts? That was where it all must have started. Everyone involved was from Harding Handicrafts. What had happened had happened to—and in—Harding Handicrafts. Whatever remained to be discovered was—inevitably—to be discovered in the offices of Harding Handicrafts. She must go there at once. She should not have stayed away for so long.

"This is good.'' Simone pushed aside her coffee cup, gathered up her handbag, and stood. "I shall return now and inform Lydia and Vernon that they may book you on the flight tonight. Then they will telephone Olive that you are coming that she may meet you.''

"Oh, not tonight,'' Karen protested. "It's too soon.''

"But, Kaa-ren, it is better soon.'' Simone frowned. "Tomorrow then? In the morning.''

"Make it the afternoon," Karen said. "I'll need *some* time to get myself organized. This is all quite sudden."

"It is a wise decision." Simone nodded. "We will all be most pleased for you. You will like it there so much that perhaps you will stay longer than only two weeks. You must feel free to do so."

Already the length of her stay was beginning to extend, Karen noted. Undoubtedly, Olive would have her own ideas—or orders—regarding the number of activities with which to occupy—and bemuse—a visitor. It would be easier to get there than to get away. Not that there was any need to worry about that, she had no intention of going. She had simply to seem compliant, while carrying out delaying action.

"It's very kind of Lydia and Vernon to be so thoughtful. I must thank them." Karen rose. "Perhaps you can give me a lift to the office."

"Kaa-ren." Simone seemed taken aback. "They will understand that you are grateful. This is not necessary."

"Perhaps not," Karen said, "but I'd prefer to thank them personally. Besides, I want to speak to them about work. The tea-set is ready for first firing."

"You should not concern yourself with this now." Simone glanced surreptitiously at her watch. "There will be time enough later."

"But I insist." Karen moved forward inexorably, watching Simone back away in confusion. "You needn't worry about my getting back. I'll walk."

"Yes—No—But—" Simone glanced at her watch again, with a trace of desperation. "There is much to be done at the office today, and—"

"I'll try not to get in anyone's way." There was no time for compassion. Simone must be dealt with as ruthlessly as Simone had been prepared to deal with her. It was obvious that Simone was now anxious to get back to the office and report her success. By taking advantage of that anxiety, Karen could ensure her own entrée.

"Well—" Simone's watch was obviously relaying an urgent summons, she was weakening visibly. "Perhaps—"

"I know you want to get back," Karen said. "You and Derek have an appointment—haven't you?—with Dr. Feltham." The appointment had been made with Derek alone, but Simone rose to the bait.

"This is true. We must hurry. He may be there now."

"Quite possibly." Karen allowed herself to be herded towards the front door. "But Derek can keep him occupied until you get there. I heard him say that he'd talk to him this morning." Which was as far as she intended to go towards admitting that she knew the appointment had been with Derek and not with both of the Conways.

"Oh yes, Derek will talk to him." Simone's mouth twisted. "Derek is very good at talking. One must know him indeed well before learning that it is not always wise to listen to what he says."

Karen caught up her handbag from the hall table and collected her coat from the cupboard in somewhat abashed silence. She and John had sometimes speculated on the intricacies of the Conways' private life, but she was not prepared for any sudden intimate revelations. She had enough problems of her own to think about right now.

"I listened," Simone said. "Derek talks beautifully, and

my English was not very good at that time. Also, he was very handsome. So I listened—and I believed.''

No answer was really required—not that Karen had one to give. She swung open the front door and allowed Simone to precede her, while she paused to lock the door behind them. Simone waited for her, still talking, almost as though to herself.

"One believes so much more when one is young— before one has had time to learn." Simone shrugged, forgiving her younger self. "This is natural."

"Of course it is," Karen agreed—too warmly. But Simone did not appear to notice.

"What Derek says is not always true." Simone slipped behind the wheel of her car and switched on the ignition, barely waiting for Karen to open the door and get into the passenger seat before she started the car moving. "This is why I must be there. I am not sure that everyone always understands what he means to be saying. I think of myself, and I think perhaps everyone is as—as—"

"Gullible," Karen supplied.

"This is so." Simone glanced at her. Tyres squealed as she took a turn too sharply. "This is why—" She raised her hand from the steering-wheel in a supplicating gesture, "I must be there with him."

"You might have a better chance of making it in time," Karen said faintly, "if you just concentrated on driving."

"This is so." Simone straightened and gave her full— rather grim—attention to the road ahead.

CHAPTER 17

NOT surprisingly, Lydia was in Vernon's office. Lydia was more often to be found in the office than in her home—not that one was likely to go looking for her. It was just that it was rather hard to avoid her.

"Karen, honey!" She rushed forward now, hands outstretched, not seeming to notice that Karen flinched. "I'm *so* glad to see you—and you *are* looking better. Isn't she, Vernon?"

"Much better, much better." Vernon snatched at her hand and wrung it too vigorously. "Still a bit tired-looking, though. You didn't walk here, did you?"

"Simone gave me a lift. She's parking the car now." Karen withdrew her hand, just short of pulverization.

"Good, good." Vernon exchanged glances with Lydia. They were obviously ill at ease, unsure of what her presence meant. Simone had not had time to brief them, perhaps they had not even been aware that Simone had taken it upon herself to plead their case. "How about some coffee?" Vernon suggested.

"I'd like that, thank you." She detested the company coffee, but it would give them all something to do to cover the awkwardness of the situation for a short while. She wondered which room the auditors had taken over. Perhaps she could take a quiet wander-round after the social amenities were over and find it without any necessity for asking.

Lydia spoke briefly into the intercom, despatching someone from the secretarial pool for coffee. "That won't take a minute," she assured them, turning back to face the room. "Why don't you sit down, honey?" Her manner was pleasant, but faintly absent, as though she were wondering about the reason for this unexpected visitation.

"The tea-set is coming along," Karen said. "I'm giving it a first firing today."

"You're always welcome here, Karen." Vernon was reproachful. "You don't have to bring business into it all the time."

I prefer to. If it weren't for business, they wouldn't have anything in common at all. The thought did not appear to have occurred to Vernon.

"I'm dying to see it." Lydia seemed to feel that a certain amount of enthusiasm was called for. "Those sketches you showed us were *so* cute." She pouted. "I just wish you weren't so funny about never letting anyone see work in progress. I've been longing to see how it was coming along."

The arrival of the coffee saved Karen from having to make any reply to this. Immediately behind the girl with the coffee, came Harvey.

"Karen—" He came towards her, hands outstretched. "I'm delighted to hear the news. Simone just told me."

"We're all pleased, Harvey," Lydia said. "It means the order will go out on time after all. Not that it would have made any difference," she hastened to reassure Karen, "if you hadn't felt up to finishing it. They'd just have had to wait, that's all."

"Wait? Order?" Harvey looked at them in puzzlement. "I don't think we're talking about the same thing. Hasn't Karen told you? She's agreed! She's flying to New York tomorrow. I'll talk to Olive on the telephone tonight and she can make the arrangements at that end."

"Why, honey, that's wonderful!" Lydia exclaimed.

"Very sensible," Vernon said. "Get away, that's what you need. Put a new perspective on things. *Very* sensible." His tone betrayed that they had given up all hope of her being so sensible.

"Simone persuaded her," Harvey said fondly. "She went round this morning without telling anyone and they had a real little girl-talk. Now Karen realizes that we have only her best interests at heart."

"Karen ought to have known that all along," Lydia said, a bit stiffly, not pleased that Simone had succeeded where she had failed.

"She knows it now." Vernon beamed at them all impartially. "Karen is one of the best ceramic designers in the business. All else aside, we couldn't afford to lose her. Now I'm happy to say that Vandergreit Enterprises will be proud to take her aboard as a member of their top-flight American team. She'll be a prize asset to us."

Asset stripping. A remark of John's suddenly came back to Karen. He had returned home gaunt and tired one night a few weeks ago. Listlessly, he had picked at the meal she had prepared. Lost in her own thoughts—the tea-set had just been suggested and she was beginning to see some of the shapes it should take—she had asked with absent interest about his problems and only half-listened to the answer.

Asset stripping, he had said. It was often a corollary to a takeover. Harding Handicrafts had hoped to avoid it, their position had seemed strong enough, had seemed that way even after the American crew had moved in and taken over control of the Boardroom. They had said nothing about it then, and it was usually in the early stages that the subject came up. But no, Harding Handicrafts had been lulled into a false sense of security, had basked in that sense of security for an inordinately long time—as taken-over firms reckoned time. They had even thought they were safe. Now, suddenly, it was starting.

Asset stripping. First they realized all the more liquid assets of a firm, after which they went public, thus getting a double profit from a firm that they had probably bought into quite cheaply to begin with. It was the penalty firms paid for being taken over, for not having managed their assets themselves to the maximum advantage.

It shouldn't have happened, John had also said. Harding Handicrafts should have been strong enough to fight it, but something had gone wrong somewhere. Through carelessness, mismanagement, inefficiency, too much money—the lifeblood of any company—had drained away. Vandergreit Enterprises were now justified in trying to realize something on their original investment, and then taking the company—neatly powdered-over and rouged and healthy-looking—to market for a fresh infusion of investment money to try to put it back on its feet and keep it there.

But first, asset stripping. And now it appearred that *she* was one of the assets.

". . . you'll love it there," Lydia seemed to be assuring her. In keeping with her new role, Karen judged it time for a modest demur.

"I'm really terribly grateful to you for your attitude." She lowered her lashes. "After all that's happened, I shouldn't think you'd want anything to do with anyone bearing the Randolph name—"

"Now, now," Vernon said. "That's all in the past. We must look to the future." He seemed to have written off quite a large amount of money quite quickly.

"Honey, just you don't even *mention* such a thing!" Lydia cried.

Not with the auditors lurking somewhere around a corner. Karen smiled faintly and sipped her coffee.

An uneasy hush had fallen over the room. The atmosphere was that of suspended action. There was rather the same feeling in the air as there was when some former typist came back to visit, bearing her young progeny. After the initial ooh-ing and aah-ing there was increasingly little to say, and gradually those who had not known her, or known her slightly, retreated to their own typewriters and lightly began to clatter away, joined by others who slid from the group until, eventually, only those trapped within the immediate radius were still awkwardly trying to make conversation while obviously longing to get back to their own work.

The Board had no typewriters to retreat to, but they were just as obviously wishing that she would go away and let them get back to whatever work they had.

But there was another feeling in the room, as well. A

dark positive stirring of unease—perhaps of guilt. Someone wanted her to go very badly—and not just from this room, but from this town and from this country. She looked around casually, trying to pinpoint the source of the emanations of unease.

"Ah, Kaa-ren, you are here." The door opened and Simone bustled into the room, shattering the delicate atmosphere. She turned her head from one to another, and gave a short satisfied nod, registering those present. "That is good."

"We've just been telling Karen how glad we are that she's changed her mind," Vernon said.

"And I think we owe Simone a vote of thanks." Harvey beamed at Simone—it looked as though he were going to go into another one of his embarrassing eulogies. Except that they never seemed to embarrass Simone, Lydia and Vernon were apparently unaware that there was anything to be embarrassed about, and Derek was usually just annoyed that they were never directed at him.

"Yes," Harvey went on, "Simone has a real gift for dealing with people. If she weren't already too valuable to us on the accountancy side, I'd be ready to nominate her for Director of Personnel."

"Oh, she's a girl of many talents, all right." Was there a trace of asperity beneath Lydia's honeysuckle drawl. "Would y'all like to have some coffee, too?"

"For me, no." Simone smirked virtuously. "I must return to work. I merely looked in to see that Kaa-ren was here safely."

Did she expect me to run away? It was an interesting thought, made even more interesting by the realization that there was a sound of running footsteps outside. Running down the corridor, coming towards Vernon's office.

Lydia's head lifted and turned towards the doorway. The others did not seem to notice anything amiss. Simone, Harvey and Vernon were all too busy admiring each other. They seemed taken aback when, after a perfunctory tap, the door burst open and Jill rushed into the room.

"Vernon," she cried, "have you seen—?"

"What's all the rush?" Vernon asked. "What's the matter?"

Of them all, perhaps Karen was the only one to realize that Jill had broken off so abruptly because she had noticed Simone was in the room. But then, she knew Jill and her reactions better than the others.

"Dr. Feltham." Jill had taken a deep breath and was speaking with careful control. She avoided Simone's eyes. "Have you seen Dr. Feltham? It's urgent."

"Dr. Feltham will be in Derek's office," Simone said with bland assurance. "I have heard them make the appointment. You will find him there."

"No," Jill said. "He isn't there. I—I've just looked in—" Inadvertently her gaze crossed Simone's.

Simone stopped smiling. She opened her mouth as though to protest, closed it again, moved one hand in a brief gesture of repudiation, then moved swiftly towards the door.

"No!" Jill said. "Don't let her go down there!" But Simone was already on her way.

Harvey took one look at Jill's face, then turned and dashed out of the door after Simone.

"What in hell is going on here?" Vernon asked plaintively.

Lydia appeared to have taken in the situation more quickly, at least she knew that something was seriously wrong, even though she wasn't sure what it might be. She moved to the intercom again and Karen heard her ordering a call to be put out over the tannoy for Dr. Feltham to report to the Managing Director's office if he were in the building. That done, she too turned to Jill, waiting for her answer.

"It's Derek," Jill said. "He's—"

A sharp high scream, in a voice barely recognizable as Simone's, echoed down the corridor. Then a second scream, and then silence.

"Would Dr. Feltham please report to the Managing Director's office..." The muted metallic voice still managed to convey urgency. *"Would Dr. Feltham please report to the Managing Director's office immediately."*

"I'm afraid it's too late," Jill said. "He was lying there half sprawled across his desk. I'm afraid he's dead."

"Oh, poor Simone!" Lydia turned and hurried from the room.

"But—what happened?" Vernon persisted, looking nervously after Lydia, obviously torn between following her and staying where he was in the hope that he might learn more.

"I don't know," Jill said. "I didn't go all the way into the office. I opened the door and just stepped inside when I saw him lying there. So still. I spoke and he didn't answer." She ducked her head guiltily. "I—I'm afraid I panicked. I—I just backed out of there and ran."

"Now you mustn't let it upset you," Vernon hastened to be comforting. "Any young girl would have done the same."

But not Jill. It was completely unlike Jill. Karen found

that she had stopped believing the story. Something else was wrong—or missing. She tried to catch Jill's eye, but Jill was no more anxious to cross gazes with her than she had been with Simone.

"Now, I think we have some brandy here—" Vernon went to what he called his "hospitality cabinet" and opened it. "Purely medicinal, you understand." The words seemed to recall something to him. "Where the devil is that doctor?" He looked round irritably.

"Hadn't you better call the police?" Karen suggested. She stopped just short of adding, "*now*," which might have sounded a bit vindictive.

"No! No!" The suggestion appeared to astound Vernon. "What would we want to do that for?"

"It's customary in England when someone has been found dead."

"But—" he floundered. "There must be some mistake—"

"I'm afraid not," Jill said.

"But we can't—"

Suicide? Accident? Misadventure? No, they most probably couldn't. Would the police be likely to contemplate such a verdict twice in a row? In fact, had they even accepted it the first time? For Grace?

"We must talk." Vernon came to a decision. "As soon as the others come back, we'll have a conference."

It was highly unlikely that Simone was going to be in any mood for a conference, but he hadn't appeared to realize that as yet. Karen noticed that he had specified "*when*" the others returned. Evidently he had no intention of joining them. Was it because of some notion of delicacy—or just squeamishness?

"I don't think we ought to call anyone . . . just yet."
Unexpectedly Jill joined in.

"Right! That's right!" Vernon turned gratefully towards
this unlooked-for support. "We don't want to do anything
hasty."

Jill wouldn't meet the eyes of either of them. Her face
was shuttered. For the first time, Karen found that she
could not read Jill's expression, and had no idea what was
going on behind the bland mask. She knew only one thing:
Jill was hiding something.

"There's probably some perfectly reasonable explanation." The words slid out glibly; Vernon seemed unaware
that he had used them before, and in what context. One
emergency at a time was enough for him—and the current
one took precedence.

There was a knock on the door and they all turned
towards it with relief.

"Come in," Vernon bellowed. "Come in." He started
for the door, as though suspecting unwarranted shyness on
the part of anyone who bothered to knock. The door opened
before he reached it.

"This *is* the Managing Director's office?" Ian Feltham
came into the room hesitantly, although the door had been
plainly labelled on the outside with a brass plaque. "You
wanted me? I heard the announcement. It's a bit unnerving
to be greeted by your own name just as you enter a strange
building."

Was he a little too insistent that he had just arrived? Karen
glanced sharply at Jill, whose face was still giving nothing
away. But Jill, she knew with sudden insight, would protect
Ian Feltham, would even lie for him, if necessary.

"Dr. Feltham," Vernon said thankfully. "You're wanted—needed—in another office. Down the hall." He looked to Jill, she looked firmly away. This was one task Vernon was not going to delegate easily.

"What's wrong?" Ian asked. He made an abortive movement towards the door. "Perhaps I should get my bag?"

"I don't think that will be necessary," Jill said in a strained voice.

Ian glanced at her sharply, she wouldn't look at him either. "Where is this office?" he asked Vernon.

"Down the hall—" Vernon waved a hand hopefully, then gave up. "I'll show you," he said.

They left the office, Ian walking more rapidly than Vernon, seeming to urge Vernon along. Automatically, Karen moved to follow them. Jill's hand on her arm stopped her. She turned to meet Jill's anguished eyes.

"Wait," Jill said. "I want to talk to you."

Since she was already patently talking to her, Karen raised an eyebrow. And waited.

"Karen, don't—don't jump to conclusions—" Jill seemed to be having difficulty speaking. "I—I may be imagining things. I didn't get a clear look at all—"

"What is it?" Karen tensed.

"When I opened the door to Derek's office—" Jill swallowed. "Just before I saw Derek, I saw—I thought I saw—out of the corner of my eye. You know the way you do—more of an impression than seeing anything, really." She hesitated.

"I know," Karen said tightly. "Go on."

"I saw—" Jill looked miserable. "That is, I thought I saw—John. Just going out the connecting door between the two offices."

149

CHAPTER 18

NO one had thought it strange that she should wish to go home right away. No one had seemed to notice it at all in the confusion. She was, basically, so much on the periphery of Harding Handicrafts that it was possible that they had not even missed her. The creative force came and went; most of them working, as she did, from their own homes, only reporting to the offices for meetings or instructions. The office staff and management structure functioned as a self-sufficient entity, independent of the creative force, without which it could not have functioned at all.

But the house was empty. She rushed quickly through all the rooms, then wandered through them again—more slowly, as though John were a parcel which might blend into the background and be overlooked in the first hurried search.

Of course Jill hadn't been sure. "*An impression*," she had said. The certainty had been Karen's. She had to face the fact that it might have been born only of hope. Jill was not to blame in any way for this overpowering feeling of depression, this sense of isolation and abandonment.

It was with relief that she heard the doorbell ring, even though she knew it could presage no development of any real concern to her. John had his own key.

She had not expected to find Simone there, Harvey hovering protectively at her elbow. Karen stepped back involuntarily and they took it as an invitation and moved into the house. Simone walked slowly, not appearing to focus on anything, like a sleepwalker, unaware of her surroundings.

"I hope this is all right, Karen," Harvey said. "I just couldn't think of where else to take her. Not back to her own place—the way things are. And I couldn't bring her home, with Olive not there—"

Poor Harvey, so endlessly concerned with the conventions. As though anyone would suspect him of taking advantage of Simone at a time like this. Still, his code refused to allow him to place her in what even the wildest Victorian prude might consider a compromising situation.

"Come in," Karen said belatedly, stepping still farther back. They followed her into the living-room.

"I knew you wouldn't mind." Harvey shepherded Simone gently towards the wing chair and urged her into it. "After all, out of everybody, you're the one who can understand most what Simone is going through. I mean, you've both—" He broke off abruptly.

You've both lost your husbands. Harvey meant well, but his best friend could never accuse him of tact.

"I'm awfully sorry—" He began to compound the offence by apologizing profusely. "I didn't mean—"

"It's all right." The only way to stop Harvey was to

divert him. "Where's Lydia? I should have thought she'd have come with you." She usually *was* around trying to be a comfort to someone.

"Oh, Lydia." For a moment, a grin broke through the consternation on Harvey's face. "She had to take Vernon home. He came down to Derek's office with the doctor, took one look, and fainted. Lydia had her hands full, so I—" He broke off again, looking anxiously at Simone's immobile face.

"Of course I'd have taken care of you, anyway," he assured her.

"Perhaps Simone would like a drink," Karen offered. That remote woman sitting so silently, so unlike the usually volatile, voluble Simone, unnerved her.

"I don't think so," Harvey said. "I've given her a drink. Well, two or three. Doubles, at that. To tell the truth—" He glanced nervously at Simone before continuing with his burst of candour. "I guess she ought to be swacked to the eyeballs with the amount I've poured into her. But it doesn't seem to have had any effect at all. I guess maybe it doesn't—at a time like this."

It doesn't.

"Perhaps Simone would like to lie down for a little while." It was the only other thing she could think of to offer. They regarded the breathing effigy with concern. "And we could talk," Karen added, since Simone did not appear to be attending. She still had no idea of what had happened.

"That's not a bad idea," Harvey agreed. "Come on." He took Simone's arm. "Why don't we—?"

Simone sat listless, unseeing and unhearing. She shook off his hand as though it had been a gadfly.

Between them, they managed to get Simone, unresisting, upstairs and into the bedroom. She sat on the edge of the bed, still unaware of her surroundings, and looked up at them.

"But this is not right," she said in bewilderment. "It should not be like this."

"No," Karen said sadly. "It shouldn't be, but it is." Fellow-feeling for Simone was something she had never expected to experience, but circumstances alter—and alter rapidly. She recognized the bewildered incredulity that had settled over Simone—it was an old acquaintance of hers.

"Just lie back, dear." Harvey pushed tentatively at Simone's shoulder. "Try to get a little sleep."

"Sleep? But I have not long been up—" Simone looked at her watch incredulously. "It is not even noon yet. Can this be true?"

"That's right," Harvey said. "It's still pretty early, but it's been a—"

Busy day. Karen and Simone exchanged brief glances—momentarily united in exasperation. Harvey's grasp of chichés was international.

Simone leaned back against the pillows and closed her eyes. "Perhaps I rest a moment," she murmured wearily.

"We'll be downstairs if you should want anything." The best kindness one could offer Simone right now was to remove Harvey before he blundered further . . .

"She's in a terrible state—terrible," Harvey whispered hoarsely, following Karen down the stairs. "I've never seen her like this before."

"Well, you wouldn't have, would you?"

"What? Oh. Oh, I see what you mean. No. Poor

Simone.'' He sank into a chair and mopped his brow. ''I could use that drink she didn't take now.''

Karen got him one and one for herself.

''Thanks.'' He gulped at it and settled back. ''What a terrible thing to have happen to such a nice pair of kids. It's a nightmare.''

She had been in a nightmare of her own recently—still was—but the immediate crisis was most vivid to Harvey. Perhaps he had even forgotten that John was still missing—and the bearer bonds, so far as he knew. Or perhaps he had simply tucked it all away in a corner of his mind to be dealt with when the auditors discovered it and began asking awkward questions. At which time, presumably, it would become the most important issue again and receive due priority.

Or *was* John still missing? Had Jill really seen him? If so, could that mean that he was on his way here to retrieve the bearer bonds—and, possibly, herself? But what of Grace? And Derek?

''Harvey—'' She looked across at him. His head was still shaking from side to side slowly as though, having set it in motion, he had forgotten to stop it again. ''Harvey, what happened to Derek?''

''Oh God!'' Harvey groaned. He took another swallow. ''It was terrible—a terrible accident. It must have been.''

''Then . . . it wasn't anything like a heart attack?''

''Heart attack?'' He was surprised. ''Where did you get that idea?''

''It's usually the first thing one thinks of.'' But there was nothing usual about the situation at Harding Handicrafts— at least, not to people like them. To the police, now, it was probably an old story—in fact, they weren't called in unless there was something badly amiss.

"No," Harvey said. "It was nothing like that. I wish to God it had been."

So did she. She had not really believed in a heart attack, it had simply been a theory she had clung to since Jill had brought John into this. When the police were called, would Jill feel it her duty to tell them her "impression", too?

"It's the worst thing that could possibly have happened," Harvey said. "The publicity—" He shuddered.

"Will there have to be any?" They had managed quite successfully, so far, at hushing up what had been going on. Of course a dead body was harder to gloss over than a missing one.

"We'll try to keep it quiet." Harvey mopped his brow again. "But there were too many outsiders involved. Your cousin, that doctor— Even the auditors came down to see what was going on—"

There were faint sounds from upstairs as though Simone, unable to lie still any longer, had got up and was roaming aimlessly around the bedroom. Harvey stiffened, all his attention diverted.

"She can't rest." He glanced upwards uneasily. "Do you think I ought to go up and—?"

"I think she'd rather be alone for a while," Karen said firmly. "You were telling me about Derek—?"

"Yes." Distracted, Harvey turned back to her. "You know we're always experimenting with new lines, testing new ideas?" He was the harassed Sales Director once more.

"I know." John had occasionally brought some of the test lines home and they had played about with them, trying them out to check whether they were as simple as they ought to be; whether the line could retain interest or whether it would be more the sort of thing to be picked up as an impulse buy and subsequently regretted by the customer, thus creating a vague residue of bad will for Harding Handicrafts. Some lines had worked very well and gone on to be good steady sellers, some had shown problems early on and been quietly dropped before getting to the marketing stage.

"We're in the final tryouts of a new photographic Hobby Kit," Harvey said. "For amateur photographers, a simplified developing process. Hell, it's got chemicals in it—what doesn't have, these days? You can't develop film without chemicals. But it isn't for kids, it's aimed at the adult end of the market. They're supposed to have sense enough not to—"

She remembered that kit. John had been dubious about it. *"I don't like kits with chemicals,"* he had said. *"Most of our customers are people with children, and it's too easy to forget for a moment and put a tempting little box down where childish fingers can reach it while Mother dashes to answer the doorbell or the telephone. Apart from which, I don't like chemicals at all. I feel it's taking Harding Handicrafts too far away from the handicrafts field."*

But Vandergreit Enterprises had a toy-making Continental subsidiary which produced items like paint and glues for model plane enthusiasts and chemistry sets for scientifically-minded children. Thus, they had easy access to chemicals and could acquire them even more cheaply by bulk buying. *Rationalizing our holdings*, Vernon had called it.

"Wasn't that the kit you had so much controversy over? Something about a sort of pseudo-cyanide?"

"Damn it!" Harvey exploded. "Anyone using that kit with reasonable care *couldn't* have harmed themselves with it."

More restless movements upstairs. Was that a drawer opening and closing?

"The stupidity of it!" Harvey raged. "The carelessness! I suppose he was thinking about that new girl-friend of his instead of paying attention to what he was doing."

She had not heard anything about a new girl-friend before. Not that that meant anything. With Derek, there was always a new girl-friend.

"He must have got the chemical crystals mixed up with the sugar." Harvey shook his head. "There was a cup of coffee on his desk—hell, all over his desk. He must have knocked it over when he fell. The way I figure it, maybe he knocked over the sugar earlier, and maybe the crystals, too—he *couldn't* have dipped his spoon into them instead of the sugar bowl. But if he spilled everything and tried to scoop up just the sugar—you English being so thrifty—"

"That doesn't sound very likely." Karen shook her own head. Not even when the sugar shortage was at its worst would any sensible person have risked ingesting sugar mixed with an unknown chemical. An unsweetened cup of coffee would have been preferable.

"You don't think so, huh?" He did not seem surprised that he had not convinced her. "Well, maybe I *was* reaching for it a bit, but there's got to be some reasonable explanation—"

"You don't think anyone would consider suicide?" It was the first explanation they had tried to propound for Grace.

"No—what would he do a thing like that for?" Harvey

looked momentarily regretful. "Besides, there wasn't any note."

She realized that he thought she was trying to be helpful, suggesting a theory he could put forward to the police to cover up the facts—whatever they might be. Incredibly, he even seemed to find this perfectly natural—he had no doubt at all that she was on their side. Certainly, it had not appeared to occur to him that she was secretly longing to get him out of her house—both him and Simone, as well.

"We were planning to market it in time for the Christmas trade. This means we'll have to postpone the launch, maybe for as much as a year." He looked across at her earnestly. "Do you think that will be long enough for the English public to forget, or do you think we might have to drop the line altogether?"

"I don't know," she said. He was obviously settling in for a nice long discussion. Of course he was never anxious to go home when Olive was on one of her frequent visits to the States. In fact, Harvey at a loose end was one of the occupational hazards one encountered at Harding Handicrafts. But even if he weren't willing to return home, shouldn't he at least be back at the office?

"The trouble is," he brooded, "your Press never lets anything drop. Not unless it's actionable. You pick up any newspaper and start reading an item and you'll find bits of scandal ten or fifteen years old included, just in case the public might have forgotten it. They could ruin our launch—whenever we hold it—if they do that to us."

And the Press might be even quicker than the police at adding together a drowned secretary, a poisoned sales manager and a missing executive. A realization Harvey would eventually arrive at as he followed the circuitous processes of his thoughts to their logical conclusion. Already a new uneasiness was stirring in the depths of his eyes.

"Are you sure you ought to be—?" No, that sounded too inhospitable. "I mean, you're very welcome to stay here as long as you like, of course, but don't you think you might be needed back at the office? If Vernon and Lydia aren't there, then who's handling any problems that might arise? As soon as the Press gets wind of it, they're bound to start telephoning. Someone with experience ought to be there to talk to them."

"You're right!" He struggled forward in his chair, draining his glass. "I was sort of hanging on here because I hoped Jill would be coming back. She was the first to find him and— And also, I wasn't sure whether Simone might need me again, but she seems to have settled down all right."

"Yes." There were still furtive movements upstairs, but she was not prepared to argue the point with Harvey. She just wanted to get him out of the house without further debate. "If there's anything Simone needs, I can get it for her."

Once Harvey was out of the way, she could go upstairs and see what Simone was doing.

"If you run into Jill," she added, "ask her to ring me, please." Would assigning him an errand speed his going? Although agreeing that he ought to, he seemed in no hurry to leave.

"Sure I will," he said. "I'll be glad to. In fact, I'll send her along home. My God!" He seemed struck by a new thought. "What a time to have this happen. Of course you want to do your packing. You're leaving for New York in the morning."

"I shouldn't think so now," Karen said. No need to tell

him that she had never intended going, this would be enough of an excuse to defer the trip. A deferment that could be extended indefinitely.

"You shouldn't? Why not? This has nothing to do with you. They'll want to talk to Simone, naturally. And possibly to the rest of us who were there. But not to you."

Was Harvey as dense as he seemed? Could anyone be?

"But Harvey," she reminded him gently. "I *was* there."

"That's right," he said. "Of course you were." He looked startled, as though the idea had just occurred to him. Or perhaps it was the realization that the police might want to question her, after all, and that one question would inevitably lead to another. "But you didn't know anything about it. You wouldn't be able to help us at all."

A movement behind him, beyond the french windows, drew her attention. She looked over his shoulder as he continued to expound on her lack of interest to the police, trying to keep her face from changing.

"You needn't worry," he said. "You—What was that?"

There had been a crash from upstairs. They both looked upstairs, then at each other.

"Simone!" Harvey said. "She must have fallen— Fainted—" He turned and charged out of the room, obviously expecting her to follow.

As he disappeared, Karen crossed to the french windows and threw them open. The figure which had retreated out of sight came forward again.

"Get inside quickly," she said. "Before anyone sees you. Into the studio. I'll be with you in a minute."

She paused and closed the french windows behind her husband.

CHAPTER 19

THERE was silence upstairs. With luck, she might be able to snatch a conversation with John before Harvey came back. With *real* luck, Simone might decide she ought to return to the office with Harvey to help restore order.

Meanwhile, John had gained the studio and was waiting inside, the door standing ajar. She hesitated, another moment, listening. Still no sound elsewhere in the house—which must mean that Simone was neither unconscious nor hurt, in either of which cases, Harvey would have been bellowing for her. She crossed to the studio and stepped inside, closing the door behind her.

"Karen!" John came forward and seemed surprised when she evaded his arms. "What's the matter?"

"The bonds are in the cupboard." She decided on shock tactics. "Right where you left them!"

"Why shouldn't they be?" He seemed even more surprised. "Karen, what's wrong?"

"Wrong?" She felt tears brimming in her eyes and blinked them back. "Oh, nothing, nothing at all. What *could* be wrong? My husband simply disappears off the face of the earth and I was foolish enough to get upset about it. Neurotic of me, wasn't it?"

"Disappears?" He stared at her blankly. "What do you mean—disappears?"

"You left here last Friday morning and I haven't seen or heard of you since. You disappeared."

"Not heard. But I gave Grace a message for you—"

"Grace is dead."

"Dead? Grace?" His shock was genuine and unmistakable. His eyes were blank with it, his face white and drawn. He had not known, could not have known—he was not able to dissemble that well. Deep inside her, she felt muscles she hadn't even known were tense begin to relax.

"But how? What happened?"

"Grace drowned," she said. "They found her in Millrace Pond, behind the driving wheel of the company car. The police are investigating now."

"But Grace couldn't drive."

"There are several people—" Karen lowered her voice carefully—"prepared to swear that they had been giving her lessons."

"And the police—" He seized on the next most notable point. "What else are the police investigating?"

"Not you." She met his eyes squarely. "Not yet. The Board have done everything they could to avoid it. They wanted to give you the benefit of the doubt until—"

"*Me?*" Again he was incredulous. "*Benefit of the doubt?*" She watched his face change as the meaning sank in and he cursed quietly but powerfully for a few moments before pulling himself up sharply.

"So that's it," he said. "Clever of them. It might even have worked."

"It *did* look bad," she said. "You were missing, and the bearer bonds were missing, and—until yesterday, we thought Grace was missing with you."

"*You* thought that?"

"I—" The nightmare rushed back at her. "I didn't know. You hadn't said anything about staying away. And there was no message, no letter—"

"Grace had the message—" His face was dark. "I gave it to her at the airport when I—I discovered something that meant I had to return to Brussels immediately. I gave her a message for you, and one for Vernon—" He stopped, looking at her as though he still wondered how much he ought to tell her.

"The company car," he said thoughtfully. "*My* car."

She nodded.

"So that's why it wasn't in the airport parking lot where I left it. I thought Vernon might have had it collected for some reason. Grace was going to take the train home—*because* she couldn't drive."

"And Derek." This was something else she had to tell him, had to find out for herself. "Did you see Derek Conway this morning? You *were* at Harding Handicrafts earlier, weren't you?"

"I looked in—briefly," he admitted. "I didn't want to stay, nor did I particularly want to be seen. I think it will be as well if no one knows I'm back yet."

So Jill was right—she *had* glimpsed him this morning. Just leaving Derek's office, she had said.

"But you *did* see Derek?"

"Only just. That is, I saw him, but he didn't see me. He was head down on the desk taking a quick nap—it wasn't the first time I've discovered him like that. But it wasn't the moment to call him on it. I slipped away and left him to it."

"Derek wasn't asleep," she told him. "He was dead."

"Dead?" He moved to a chair and sat down. "Are you sure?"

"Jill found Derek—" Instinctively, she did not wish to mention that Jill had seen him, too. "It seems Derek had been fooling around with the new Hobby Kit—the photographic one—and must have been careless. The theory is that he spilled some of the chemicals into his coffee in some way and drank it without noticing what he'd done—"

"Then he was dead when I saw him?"

"Yes. Another—" deliberately, she put vocal quotation marks around the word—"another 'accident'."

"Another . . . accident." His face told her nothing this time. Perhaps the shock of learning about Grace had inured him to all other shocks.

"Don't you think you might tell me what this is all about?" she suggested.

"I don't know." He smiled ruefully. "I didn't want you involved."

Involved. She bit down on a laugh which would have been hysterical. "Involved? I've been in the front line of fire for a week—and I don't know what the battle is all about. I didn't even know there was a war on."

"You're right. You ought to know." He glanced at the window-seat cupboard and turned back to her. "What about a cup of coffee and some food? I haven't stopped too much for food lately. I've been moving fast and hard. We can talk while we eat.''

''All right.'' She heard the squeak of the cupboard door as she moved away. Perhaps he simply wanted her out of the way while he transferred the bonds to a new hiding place—one she wouldn't know about, but she didn't care. He had come back. That was enough to be going on with.

As she closed the studio door behind her, she realized that she had forgotten Harvey and Simone for the past few minutes. A very dangerous thing to do when they were both upstairs and might descend to discover John with the bearer bonds at any moment.

If he were to be found now, everyone would immediately assume that he had come to collect the bonds again. Worse, they might imagine that he had had something to do with Derek's death. John had to walk back into Vernon's office at Harding Handicrafts and place the bonds on Vernon's desk before his innocence would be believed. Then he could explain why he had taken the bonds and why he had been gone for so much longer than expected. He *had* a good explanation, hadn't he? She could judge that for herself— she was going to be the first to hear it.

That is, if Harvey didn't come down and interrupt them.

She hesitated, looking up the stairs. But there was still silence up there. She might have been fooled into thinking the house empty, had she not known better. How long would Harvey stay out of the way? Long enough to allow John to have something to eat and leave again?

Perhaps—if she moved swiftly enough. She turned and whirled into the kitchen, put the kettle on the gas and, quickly but silently, set a tray. Sandwiches—she got out the bread and went to the fridge. Jill had bought cold cuts at some point, she was certain, and there was cheese, butter . . . Transferring them to the tray, she paused, something nagging at her consciousness.

Something wrong . . . something odd . . . She turned back to the fridge and opened it again, letting her gaze rove thoughtfully over its contents. Then she realized what was wrong.

The egg custard Simone had brought for her days ago. It had spoiled—curdled, with a thin evil-looking fluid covering a surface pitted like the craters of the moon. Hastily, guiltily, she closed the door again quickly. Not that Simone was likely to come creeping up behind her and make a scene because her gift had been unappreciated. Simone had too many problems of her own now to worry about a little thing like that.

Nevertheless, as she moved back to pour the coffee, something flickered tantalizingly at the edge of her consciousness. Something that sparkled, then extinguished itself just as she reached out to capture it.

Let it go. If it were really important, it would come back to her later. She picked up the tray and started back to the study.

"Why, Karen—" Harvey, descending the stairs, caught her crossing the hall. "That's awfully nice of you, but you shouldn't have bothered. Here, let me—" He took the tray from her.

"It was no bother." There was nothing for it, but to try to bluff through, hoping that John wouldn't open the studio door and give himself away. "I hope you like cheese."

"Love it. So does Simone." He frowned slightly. "But, Karen, you haven't put out a cup for yourself."

"Well, no. I—I don't really want anything—"

"Oh, come on now, don't be coy." He gave her one of the meaningful looks she always dreaded. What was she supposed to understand this time?

"You know, don't you? When you didn't come up with me, I told Simone you must have guessed and were being tactful."

"Guessed? Tactful?" Her bewilderment was genuine and Harvey must have realized it.

"About us," he explained. "Simone and me. Oh, it had to come out sooner or later. Of course, the way things are at the moment, we'll have to wait for a decent period of mourning—but we'd have had to wait for divorces, anyway. Oh, it's a sad thing about Derek—in fact, it's terrible. But I have to admit that it simplifies things a bit. There'll only have to be one divorce now, instead of two, and I know Olive will be reasonable. She always wanted to stay back in the States anyhow. But Derek might have decided to put up a fight for Simone—and I wouldn't blame him. Much as he neglected her, he knew a good thing when he saw one and—"

"Har-vee—" Simone appeared at the head of the stairs. "You are talking too much."

"I guess I am, honey." He glanced up at her fondly. "But I'm so proud and happy, I can't help wanting the world to know. And I want you to know, Karen—" he faced her earnestly, still holding the tray—"I'm delighted that you're the first of our friends to find out. I have always held you in the highest regard and—"

"Har-vee—" Simone moved down the stairs slowly. "You may put the tray down now. I do not think it is required."

"Sure, honey, sure." He set the tray down on the coffee table and straightened up, beaming at her devotedly.

Simone and Harvey—why should anyone be surprised? It was logical, even natural, that they should have found each other. Both married to partners who left them alone for long stretches at a time—why should they not have turned to each other for companionship and comfort? And, having found it, why should they not wish to perpetuate it? Olive and Derek had only themselves to blame.

And yet, Karen found herself filled with a strange uneasiness. They were both smiling expectantly at her now. Surely they didn't expect congratulations? Had they actually managed to forget Derek?

"Well . . . this *is* a surprise . . ." She hoped her voice didn't sound as dubious to their ears as it did to hers. "I hope you'll be very happy."

"I truly believe we will," Harvey affirmed. "I can tell you, I've been walking on air since this little lady consented to be my—"

"Har-vee," Simone interrupted. "You are talking too much again. You are boring Kaa-ren."

"Oh no," Karen denied. "I'm not bored." She was beset by quite a lot of emotions at the moment, but boredom was not one of them.

"There now!" Harvey turned to Simone. "You see—"

"And I certainly never suspected a thing," Karen went on, realizing that, even as she said it, it had abruptly ceased to be true.

The flicker at the edge of her consciousness brightened, projecting a double image at her: two refrigerators, two doors opening, two lights going on inside, illuminating the contents. The double images shimmered for an instant longer—the top shelves, the contents of the top shelves, so alike and yet so unlike—before merging into one: curdled, separated milk. In the bottle in Grace's fridge, in an egg custard in her own. Custard given to her by Simone.

"*Simone's been using up some extra milk,*" Derek had said.

"Derek talks too much," Simone had said.

There had been no extra milk in Grace's flat—*and there should have been*. Grace, expecting to return on Sunday night, would have left instructions for the milkman to resume delivery after the weekend. There had been no extra milk. Someone must have countermanded those instructions—someone who knew Grace would not be returning. Someone who had searched Grace's flat at leisure. Someone accustomed to thinking in numbers who would have realized what too much milk might have given away. Someone who had left a note for the milkman to cease delivery again—probably investigation would turn up the milkman to confirm that. Someone who had thriftily abstracted the extra bottles and, equally thriftily, had made use of them.

Simone.

Moreover, who had been the first to insinuate that John and Grace had run away together? Who, with sly cruelty masquerading as sympathy, had insisted upon such a certainty, persuading Lydia and Vernon that the theory was fact? Who, in the final analysis, had been in the best position herself to embezzle unsuspected?

Simone.

Karen hoped that her expression had not altered too drastically. Certainly, Harvey continued to regard her with a pleased amiability, but—had Simone's eyes narrowed a tri-fle? Involuntarily, Karen took a step backwards, fighting an overwhelming instinct to turn and run.

But there was nowhere to run. She could not lead them into her studio and betray John, sheltering there. Or was he still there? Had he sent her to the kitchen to get her out of the way while he disappeared again?

"But you are so clever, Kaa-ren," Simone said. "Are we really to believe that you did not know about us?"

"No, I didn't," Karen said. "Honestly. You were both so discreet that I never imagined such a thing. Not for an instant."

"This is what I am telling Har-vee," Simone said. "We have been most forbearing, most discreet. No one could guess. Why, then, did you not come upstairs with Har-vee when he feared I had fallen? If it was not that you were being tactful and wished to allow us some time alone together, what then was it?"

"Why, I—I thought you might want some coffee." Karen moved forward, frantically gesturing towards the tray, trying to direct their attention to it—and away from the studio door, which was slowly opening.

"I do not think so." Simone twitched her shoulders impatiently. "You are upsetting me, Kaa-ren. Always I have believed you are so honest and open—now you are being as devious as Lydia. Why will you not tell me the truth? Is it because you are protecting someone else? That is the sort of thing you would do, Kaa-ren. That I could believe."

"Why don't we take our coffee out into the garden?" The studio door was distinctly ajar now, a hovering figure just discernible through the aperture. "It's such a lovely day, it seems a pity to stay indoors."

"But, Kaa-ren—" Simone stopped her as she was about to pick up the tray. "*Is* it our coffee? As Har-vee has pointed out, there are only two cups. You have none for yourself. Or was one of the cups intended for you? I do not believe you were thinking of us at all, Kaa-ren. I believe you had forgotten us. So, for whom were you making coffee, Kaa-ren? For whom did you prepare the tray?"

Simone knew. Furthermore, Simone was not surprised by the knowledge. It was more as though she had been expecting something like this. Even now her head was turning, her eyes unerringly seeking the studio door.

"Will you not come out and join us, John?" Simone invited. "Or shall we come in there and join you?"

There was no response. The figure disappeared from view, the door swung open a fraction wider.

"I think we will go in there," Simone decided. "No, Kaa-ren, do not bother about the coffee. The time for such social manners has ended. You will go in first, open the door wide, and both stand where I can see you before Harvee and I shall enter."

Karen abandoned her attempt to pick up the coffee tray and pushed open the studio door, still incredulous at what she was seeing. The time for sociability was indeed over.

Still smiling, still soft-voiced, Simone was aiming a small but very deadly-looking gun at her.

CHAPTER 20

"**O**H, now, I'm sure that won't be necessary, dear," Harvey remonstrated mildly.

"That may be true, but I am happier with it." Still smiling serenely, Simone ignored Harvey's outstretched hand and gestured with the gun. Harvey gave a shrug curiously like her own and preceded her into the studio. He glanced down as he passed her and some of the complacency slid away from him.

"Say," he said. "Isn't that Olive's gun?"

"She has no need of it," Simone said.

"No, but we thought she'd lost it. Probably when we made the move over here from the States. It's been missing a long time now."

And Simone must have had the run of Harvey's house for a long time now.

"And now it is found. As so much is found now." Simone looked around the studio, not missing the open cupboard door, the sack of clay powder, the dusting of powder on the table, the discarded plastic wrapping.

"You will give us the bearer bonds, please, John." Simone levelled the gun at him. "No—not to me. I am not to be so distracted. You may hand them to Harvey."

"It's the darndest thing about that gun. Olive looked everywhere for it when she got back from her trip. She was frantic—" Harvey accepted the bearer bonds from John, talking as though he were in the midst of a normal social gathering recounting some mildly amusing anecdote. It was Harvey at his most professionally charming, demonstrating the way he managed to keep his right hand from noticing what the left was doing. No wonder he and Simone had been so well able to conceal their relationship—not to mention their financial manipulations.

"It sounds funny, but I think Olive was really sentimental about that gun," Harvey continued conversationally, abstractedly pocketing the bonds. "Well, I suppose it *was* one of the first presents I gave her. Just after we were married. I was out on the road a lot in those days, and she was nervous about staying home alone—"

"Let Karen go!" John slashed rudely through the thin facade of civilization Harvey was projecting with his own self-hypnosis. "I haven't discussed any of this with her at all. She doesn't know a thing."

"Oh, come now—" Harvey began, pained. "There's no need to talk like that. We're not monsters—"

"I think Kaa-ren *does* know," Simone said gravely. "I think she is intelligent enough to decipher the situation for herself."

"Yes," Karen agreed. "I'm paying attention now."

And, more than paying attention, she was actively

173

attempting to calculate their chances of survival. They were not wildly encouraging.

In the first place, no one even suspected Harvey and Simone. With Simone's husband newly dead, they would never think of looking for Simone here rather than at her own home. In fact, in all the contingent confusion, no one would think of coming here at all. Probably not even Jill. Jill would be concerned with Ian Feltham—it could be hours before she thought of returning to home base. She had no way of suspecting that anything might be wrong here. On the contrary, she would imagine her stricken cousin safely out of the fray, no longer to be worried about. She would be caught up in the current crisis at Harding Handicrafts, and if she thought of Karen at all, it would be to store up interesting sidelights to recount later. Jill could not know that there was not to be a ''later.''

''I am sorry, Kaa-ren,'' Simone said. ''But you have been most foolish. You could be on your way to New York now, thousands of miles away. I liked you, and you were of value to the company. It was most remiss of you not to have taken the flight we arranged for you. You could be safely out of it all—''

''While you murdered my husband,'' Karen said. ''As you murdered Grace, as you murdered your own husband.''

''No!'' Harvey protested. ''No, Karen, you mustn't think that. It isn't true. Grace was an accident. Simone explained to me—''

''Did she?'' John asked. ''Perhaps she'd like to explain to us, then. I'd be very interested to know what explanation she could offer.''

Simone shrugged, but her eyes narrowed dangerously.

"It was an accident," Harvey insisted. "You don't think a warm, sweet person like Simone could do a thing like that to another human being—?" He faltered before their implacable gaze. "Do you?"

With a shrug as eloquent as any of Simone's, Karen looked away from the spectacle of Harvey wrapping the shreds of his infatuation around him to try to ward off the cold winds of reality.

"There was trouble with the steering gears of the car," Simone said abruptly. "You are knowing this, Kaa-ren. John is passing the garage bill on his expenses recently."

"The bill was for having the steering *fixed*," John said. "And what were you doing in the car, in any case? That car should have been in the airport parking lot—where I left it."

"I had come to meet the plane," Simone said. "There was urgent news that you should know at once. I had come by train in order that I might drive back with you. But you did not come."

"No," John said. "As I was leaving the Brussels office, I picked up a couple of files by mistake, along with my own papers. I found them just before the plane landed and a lot of things suddenly began to make sense to me. I told Grace to take the train home and tell everyone that something had come up and I was staying longer. Then I took the next flight back to Brussels. Evidently Grace met you outside."

"I am waiting outside," Simone agreed, with another shrug. "Grace is agreeing it is silly to both take the train when we know where the spare key is concealed on the car and I am a good driver. We decide we can send the car back for you when you let us know when you are arriving." Simone paused. "*Why* did you not inform us you are returning today?"

John shook his head incredulously. "Grace didn't know enough to be a danger to you, but you couldn't take the chance, could you? You got rid of her and thought you'd get rid of me when I returned. What did you do, hit her on the head and then drive her into the pond?"

"No!" Simone's denial was too quick. "This is not true. We are quite friendly, driving along nicely, and then suddenly, as I go to turn at Millrace Pond, the steering is not right. We go into the pond, and I get out of the car and I am thinking Grace is out, too—"

"The car doors were closed," Simone had said, just after the police had pulled the car from the pond. *How had she known it then?* No one had thought to question her assurance.

"I am swimming to shore and looking around," Simone continued. "But Grace is not there. Then I am fainting and, when I recover, it is too late—"

"Don't upset yourself, dear," Harvey said quickly. "There was nothing you could do. It wasn't your fault."

Could Harvey really believe that? Or must he force himself to believe it because he was too tangled in Simone's web to attempt to extricate himself? No matter what else he discovered about her now, he had certainly been party to embezzlement and fraud. In fact, if anyone had looked at the situation rationally earlier, unblinded by loyalty to colleagues or the dust thrown in their eyes over John's absence, who in the company had been in better positions to carry out such operations and successfully conceal them from the auditors than the Financial Director and the Sales Director?

John made a sudden move, reaching for a handkerchief, and Harvey jumped nervously.

"Look dear," Harvey said, "don't you think we ought to tie them up?"

"No, Har-vee. We must not have any marks on their wrists or ankles when they are found."

"Found?" For the first time, Harvey began to look upset, as though it were just coming home to him that the things that had been happening were real and not just some little game whipped together with the aid of one of Harding Handicraft's Hobby Kits.

"You do not imagine—" Simone swept him with a look of contempt—"that we can set them free? To go and tell everyone what they have learned?"

"But, honey, maybe they'd promise not to talk—?" He looked at them pleadingly, begging them for reassurance.

Poor Harvey. Even now, he had to be liked, he had to feel that his prospective victims approved of him. Or had he still not realized where they were all heading? Did he seriously believe that he could coax a promise of silence out of them? Silence about embezzlement, fraud and two murders? And did he believe that Simone would trust such a promise, even if he were willing to?

"You do not imagine—" Simone looked even more disdainful—"that they would make such an agreement?"

"Well, I guess not." Harvey turned to them reluctantly and spread his hands. "Gee, folks, what can I say—?"

If he says, "It's been great knowing you," I shall scream, I shall howl, I shall fall about. I shall go out on an ignominious wave of laughing, shrieking hysteria. Karen took a deep breath and held it precariously.

"And do *you* imagine—" Fortunately John interrupted, addressing himself directly to Simone. "Do you seriously imagine that you can decimate the management and staff of Harding Handicrafts without bringing down a full-scale police investigation upon all of you?''

''But, John,'' Simone crooned. ''Just consider. There will now be nothing left to investigate. All will be revealed. No one will have any questions at all.''

''I haven't been idle,'' John said. ''Nor have I been silent. I've traced down those invoices with false letterheads. I've found the accommodation addresses you've been sending the cheques to in payment of the fake invoices for goods we've never received. *And* I've checked in with some of the Continental police stations.''

''Of course you would do this, John,'' Simone agreed. ''It was necessary if you were to hope that you might avoid discovery. I am sure that those police were most impressed. But I am not sure that they would believe your word alone, without further evidence. And there will be no further evidence. There are no cheques outstanding at the moment. There will be no further payments for the rental of the accommodation addresses. Even the stocks of letterhead invoices have been destroyed. It is most unfortunate for all concerned that you have chosen to act so close to the time when we were in the process of winding up our operations.''

''Banks have records,'' John said grimly. ''These things don't disappear without trace. There are always loose ends you haven't even thought of.''

''Ah, but *we* will be the ones to discover them, John. And *we* will explain to the police how we first began to grow suspicious. Very reluctantly, because we were fond of you. But gradually the discrepancies in the accounts grew too great to ignore. Har-vee and I took counsel together and worried about what we should do. Then, however, you disappear—with your secretary who, of course, must have been conspiring with you. At least, that was what we believed until her body was found. Then we felt that she might have been innocent—that she, too, had found you out and had been foolish enough to speak to you about it—alone and without witnesses. And so, you killed her—''

"That's incredible." John's face was pale. "No one will believe that."

"They will not wish to believe it, perhaps. But they will have no choice when they find—''

When they find your bodies. Karen no longer felt like laughing—not even in hysteria. It was all too likely that Simone and Harvey could get away with it. That they would carry it off, tell their lies and be believed—and live happily ever after. *While she and John—*

"It will be more better if they retain some of the bearer bonds." Dismissing them from her mind, Simone spoke to Harvey. "How much will it be necessary for them to have?"

"It will have to be a fair amount to be believable, I'm afraid, sweetheart," Harvey said. "I think a hundred thousand will do it—'' He cut off her protest. "That will still leave a hundred and fifty thousand for us."

Harvey had stopped considering them, too. For a short time, it had seemed that he might waver. But now his die was cast. Had been cast, perhaps, from the first moment he had admired Simone's "cute" little accent, from the first time Olive had rushed back to the States on one of her frequent trips, leaving him alone and longing for company. Simone had often worked late at the office while Derek was off on one of his amatory adventures—and Harvey had worked late rather than go home to an empty house. It must have begun then.

But it was ending here. Ending for herself and John. *Had ended already for Grace and Derek.*

"Here—" Harvey thrust the bonds at John. "Go on, take them." His voice grew bitter. "You were so damned anxious to before—"

"Yes, I thought that would put a spoke in someone's wheel—I wasn't sure whose at the time." John's voice radiated satisfaction, however short-lived it might prove. "The bonds had to be available if the auditors called for them. As soon as the audit was over, however, they were next on the list of profits to be snatched. What were you going to do with all the money?" He was genuinely curious. "Were you going to run away together? Or were you going to drive Harding Handicrafts right down into the ground and then buy it with the very money you'd stolen from it?"

"Take the bonds." Harvey's voice was tight. "It won't do you any good not to. Your fingerprints are all over them."

"But why did you kill Derek?" Ignoring Harvey and the bonds, John spoke across him to Simone. "I can understand that you killed Grace because you thought she knew too much about your activities. But why did you kill your own husband?"

"Now that was an accident," Harvey protested. "Derek got some chemicals from the Photographic Hobby Kit mixed into his coffee. You can't blame Simone for that. She was very upset about it. It hurt her deeply."

"*Grace is a nothing.*" That had been the time to begin suspecting Simone. Although she had recoiled from the remark as she heard it, only now did the full implication strike Karen. *Now, when it was too late.* There had always been something in Simone's attitude that marked her as dangerous—if only they had been able to read the signals. Simone had never brooked interference with her own aims. She must have smouldered silently for years under the humiliations Derek had heaped on her with his younger and prettier girls. But the last straw must have come when Derek became an active threat to her own safety. *Derek talks too much.*

"Derek talked too much," Karen repeated the thought automatically. There had been time for Simone to give Derek the coffee, already poisoned, and then come over here and give herself an alibi for the time Derek died by trying to persuade Karen to go to the States.

"That is so." Simone looked at her thoughtfully. "Derek did not know much, but he was too stupid to know how much he did know. Therefore he was dangerous because he would tell everything he knew and others would be able to make the deductions he could not. It was necessary that he should go."

"But, honey," Harvey appeared staggered by the admission, "you couldn't have done it. Why, you were terribly upset about it—you were even crying. I thought you were going to collapse when you saw his body."

"That is so." Simone spoke gravely, still to Karen. "I did not expect it to hurt so much. But at the end, it seems, one goes back to the beginning. I remembered—against my will—the way we had started out, the plans we had, the dreams—" She broke off, tears in her eyes.

So Simone was human. Or almost. Despite the tears, her hand had not wavered, the gun was still pointing at them.

"You poor kid," Harvey said feelingly. "You had plenty of provocation. He did the dirty on you all along the line. We used to wonder how you stood it."

"Well, it is done." Simone blinked and the tears were gone. She shrugged, dismissing sentimentality, dismissing weakness. "It merely remains to finish the rest of it, and then we shall be free and unsuspected."

The rest of it. She meant *them.* It was *their* lives Simone was shrugging off with the euphemism. Instinctively, Karen turned to Harvey, but he evaded her eyes.

"I suppose it has to be done," he said reluctantly.

"If we are to be secure, it must be done." Simone was firm. "And you must do it, Har-vee," she added. "I have taken care of the other two. It is for you take care of these."

"Oh, now, honey—" Harvey began to protest.

"It is necessary," Simone said. "You have gloves and I have not. You must put them on now. The only powder burns must be found on those two that the police may re-enact the scene and know that John returned for the remainder of the bonds which he had hidden and was discovered by Karen. Perhaps he wished her to go away with him— Perhaps she wished him to remain and give himself up—" Simone shrugged. "It is for the police to decide. At any rate, they quarrelled. Whether she shot him and then herself, whether he shot her and then committed suicide, whether there was a struggle for the gun and both were killed—" Again Simone shrugged.

It is for the police to decide. Their decision guided, no doubt, by judicious prods from Simone and Harvey who, safe in their guise of loyal Directors and wrapped in spurious respectability, would be free to work out their own futures at their leisure.

"I really ought to be getting back to the office, honey." Harvey was obviously willing to condone Simone's actions, but not too anxious to act himself. There was no point in hoping that he felt any compunction for them—it was just the way he was.

"Oh, Har-vee—" Simone turned towards him in exasperation—"this is typical! You—"

John lunged forward. Taking advantage of Simone's off-guard moment, he snatched for the gun.

But Harvey was quicker. He intercepted John, knocking aside the reaching hand, gaining possession of the gun himself, and stepped back.

"You're right, honey," he said. "This is the one I have to handle myself—especially if we want powder burns on them. You couldn't get that close without trouble."

She should have tried to jump Simone at the same moment John did, Karen realized. But it had happened too quickly and he had given her no warning. Now it was too late.

"Him first, I think." Harvey pulled a pair of gloves from his pocket and struggled into them. "Then we can avoid any more trouble."

"You are so clever, Har-vee," Simone purred. "It shall be as you say."

"Yeah, well, I guess I do know my way around," Harvey said. "It doesn't do to rile me. He might have hurt you—"

Such affection might have been touching—had it been directed to a more worthy recipient. Unable to stand the complacent smugness on Simone's face, Karen looked stolidly beyond her, then caught her breath, unable to believe what she was seeing.

The door was swinging silently open. Ian and Jill were standing there, with Lydia and Vernon behind them. As the door opened wider, Jill gestured for silence and they watched quietly while Harvey finished donning the gloves and brought the gun back into a businesslike position.

"You are so naïve, Kaa-ren," Simone said impatiently. "There is no point in looking over my shoulder in that way. We are not to be fooled by such an obvious trick."

"You can't get away with it," John told Harvey. "Your trail is clear halfway across the Continent—"

"*Your* trail, you mean," Harvey corrected. "I've been suspicious of your business trips for some time now—and that's what I'll tell the others. Simone and I got here just in time to see you shoot Karen and then kill yourself when you realized we'd caught you."

"You can't get away with it." By now, John had looked towards the doorway and his voice was firmer, but still cautious as he watched for another opening. "No one will believe that."

"Vernon will believe anything I tell him," Harvey said.

"Not any more!" Vernon snapped.

They all stood transfixed for an instant, then Simone turned and shrieked, which seemed to break the spell. Everyone moved at once, but Simone and Harvey were outnumbered and the struggle was brief.

"You can thank heaven that accountants have such suspicious natures," Jill said later. "As soon as they heard about Derek, they stopped checking poor Grace's petty cash and moved in on Derek's records and Simone's accounts. Once they were looking in the right places—and with no one to distract them—the picture began to emerge.

"I wanted to get back here right away and tell you. Meanwhile, the accountants notified Vernon and he thought he and Lydia should come along and apologize for some of the things they'd been thinking—''

"We met on the doorstep," Lydia continued. "We came in together, and we heard *everything*. I've never been so shocked in my life. *Harvey!* And to think we were harbouring such a snake in the grass in our bosoms!"

"Harvey has been a grave disappointment to us," Vernon admitted sadly. "And so has Simone. To think that we were grooming them both for top International Management!"

"And Olive—" Lydia mourned. "Poor dear Olive. This is going to come as a dreadful shock to her. What will she do now?"

"Perhaps—" Karen was a bit caustic, remembering the fate they had planned for her—"perhaps you can introduce her to some suitable gentleman in the New York office."

"You know—" Lydia brightened—"that's not a bad idea. There's a very charming widower—"

"I still can't get over the way Harvey treated the Company so shabbily," Vernon said. "I would have staked everything I had on his honesty."

"You almost did," John said. His glance took in the bearer bonds on the table. With the ensuing publicity, the Vandergreits would not be able to dispose of them and they would remain part of the Harding Handicrafts assets when they eventually went public. The prospective shareholders would be getting a better deal than had been intended.

"Oh, well," Vernon sighed deeply. "Life goes on, and other people must step up and fill the vacancies. Lydia and I have to be moving back to the States in a couple of weeks. We've just about worn out our welcome with your tax authorities. Any longer and they'll be treating us like natives."

"That would never do," John agreed drily.

"It certainly wouldn't! Now, we were thinking you and Karen might come along with us—"

"We won't be able to," John said firmly. "I'll be needed here to work with the accountants and try to untangle the mess. The whole thing is pretty complicated and, as yet, we've just got hold of a few pieces of the string."

"Yes, there's that, of course." Vernon accepted the idea; in no time it would seem to him that it had been his own. "And we need someone in charge we can really trust." He nodded to Lydia and she nodded back. It began to seem as though they might stay there forever, nodding to each other in mutual congratulation.

Jill stood up abruptly. "I have to get back to town," she announced. "Could someone be kind enough to give me a lift to the station?"

That brought them all to their feet. Not surprisingly, Ian decided to take her. Lydia and Vernon, finding themselves on their feet and moving towards the door, came to a conclusion.

"I suppose we ought to get along," Lydia said. "I'll telephone you tomorrow and we can take that shopping trip we missed."

"That will be fine," Karen said, feeling that she could even manage to endure Lydia's excessive friendship for the short time remaining to the Vandergreits in this country—just about.

"I suppose we *ought* to be getting along," Vernon echoed. He paused, waiting for protestations which did not come. "I suppose you two want to do some catching up, or something."

"That's right," Karen said, closing the door gratefully behind them. "We have a lot of catching up to do."